"Kaye? Are you okay?"

She heard Caleb's words through the layers of sorrow. The pain and grief rolled out of her, much like flood gates opening, and she had no control over them.

How long she cried, she couldn't say, but it seemed like hours. When sanity returned, she felt the support and comfort of Caleb's arms. This was the second time the man had held her and surrounded her with his strength.

She pulled away, wiping her face. "You'd never believe I was an efficient military officer who never once cried the entire time I was in the army. I didn't even cry when my ex told me he was filing for divorce."

"I believe you."

His response brought her gaze up to his. "Really? I took the coward's way out when I left here."

Caleb's finger lifted her chin. "I don't see a coward. I see an amazingly strong woman who has dealt with a lot of tragedy."

She searched his face, trying to see if he really meant what he said. His eyes held admiration—and something else.

Books by Leann Harris

Love Inspired

Second Chance Ranch
Redemption Ranch
Fresh-Start Ranch
*A Ranch to Call Home

Love Inspired Suspense

Hidden Deception
Guarded Secrets

*Rodeo Heroes

LEANN HARRIS

When Leann was growing up, she used to spin stories to keep herself entertained, and when she didn't like how a movie ended, she rewrote the ending—and still does.

Once her youngest child went to school, Leann gave in to her imagination and began putting those stories on a page. Since she was such a terrible typist, her husband brought home a computer, and her writing career was born.

Although she's not a native Texan, she's lived most of her adult life in Texas, married a fourth-generation Texan, and her two children are fifth-generation Texans, which is why most of her stories are set in the West or the Southwest.

She is active in her local RWA chapter and ACFW chapters. Since other writers nourished her, she wants to give to others the encouragement given her.

A teacher of the deaf (high school), she is a master composter and avid gardener, which you can look at on her website, www.leannharris.com.

A Ranch to Call Home
Leann Harris

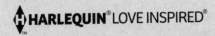

HARLEQUIN® LOVE INSPIRED®

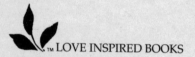

™ LOVE INSPIRED BOOKS

ISBN-13: 978-0-373-87875-8

A RANCH TO CALL HOME

Copyright © 2014 by Barbara M. Harrison

www.Harlequin.com

Printed in U.S.A.

But for you who revere my name shall the Sun of Righteousness arise with healing in His wings.
—*Malachi* 4:2

For my sweet husband,
who has supported me in all things.

My thanks to:

Steve Gander of the Mesquite Pro-Rodeo
for all his help and insights on how a rodeo operates.

Jennifer Baade and "Branigan" for their help.

Chapter One

Home. She was home.

After twelve years and a lifetime of experiences gained in the army, ex-captain Brenda Kaye was coming home to the little town of Peaster, Texas, west of Fort Worth to face—what?

Sucking in a long, steadying breath, she turned her army-surplus jeep down the dirt road that led to her family's farmhouse. When she woke early this morning, she'd felt an *urgency* to go home. She knew better than to ignore that little voice, for it had saved her life more than once. She packed her clothes and a few personal items into her vehicle, notified her apartment manager she was going to Texas and started home. She didn't call. Instead, she wanted to surprise her brother and grandfather. She didn't know what her plans for the future were, she only knew she had to go home. Now.

When the familiar white farmhouse came into view, her stomach tightened. She'd faced some intimidating fellow soldiers and hostile Iraqi men and not backed down, but the sight of her home made her heart pound and her mouth go dry. The gravel road opened up into a large area with the white-clapboard house on the right and the barn on the left, fifty or so yards away. The house had a wrap-around porch where the side kitchen door was the main door the family used.

She parked her jeep by an unknown truck but didn't see her brother's tan, two-tone F-150. Her grandfather's old, faded, green Ford pickup sat on the other side of the unknown truck. She sat for a moment and rubbed her right calf, easing the cramping there. She felt the raised scars through the khaki pant leg, a painful reminder of why she was ex-captain Kaye.

Taking a deep breath, she got out of the jeep and looked around. Home. It hadn't changed much, except for that beautiful horse trailer parked by the barn. She started up the porch steps when a voice called out, "Can I help you?" Kinda like he owned the place.

She stopped on the second riser, turned, ready to open fire, and faced a cowboy—an attractive cowboy, to be sure, but still a stranger. He stood outside the barn's double doors. His clothes—a worn chambray work shirt rolled up to his elbows, well-worn jeans, boots and work gloves—were standard garb for a working cowboy. A curl of wavy brown hair hung over his forehead as he studied her. A one-thousand-watt smile curved his mouth. "You're Joel's sister, Brenda."

Her stomach danced with awareness she hadn't felt since her divorce. She put the brakes on her schoolgirl reaction. Ex-army captains don't fall head over boot heels for a cowboy. "I'm used to going by Kaye. You'll get a response from me faster if you call me that. I was looking for Joel and my grandfather. Do you know where they are?"

He sobered. "They're at the hospital."

"What?" She fought the fear of being too late. "Why are they there?" She stepped down to the ground. Her legs felt wobbly.

The unknown man stripped off his glove and walked toward her. "Your grandfather was out in the north pasture tilling the field when the tractor's wheel slipped into a rut, flipped and pinned him underneath. Joel and I got him out, and Joel took Gramps to the hospital." He glanced up at the sun. "That was probably three hours ago."

"And they haven't called?"

"No, but your grandpa walked to your brother's truck."

Experience taught her most men thought it was their job to lie to you about any injury they suffered. The stranger continued walking toward her.

"I'm Caleb Jensen." He held out his hand. "Joel and I rodeoed together years ago when he was still on the circuit."

She shook his hand. The strong handshake spoke of a man who was sure of himself and didn't try to do a one-upmanship thing by crushing her hand. But with that subdued strength, she felt her stomach dance again. What was going on? When she looked up, she saw awareness in his eyes, and he was looking at her as if she were a woman, not an army captain.

Quickly masking her reaction, she withdrew her hand. Captain Kaye was back in control, not high school Brenda. "What hospital did they go to?"

"John Peter Smith."

Fort Worth. Did she have it in her to drive the last leg into the city? Her legs ached and were beginning to cramp, but that *urgency* inside her made it impossible to stay here and wait. She headed toward her jeep to grab her phone for a quick call to her brother. Halfway there her weakened legs gave out. Before she ended up on her dignity, Caleb caught her and gently helped her stand.

Color heated her cheeks. Before her injury, there wouldn't have been a problem driving the six hundred miles from Albuquerque, then turning around and driving to Fort Worth. Now she lived in a different world. "That drive took more out of me than I thought."

"I understand."

She walked on unsteady legs to her jeep, reached in and pulled out her cell.

"Your brother's not answering his phone. It's going to voice mail."

Rats.

"Would you like for me to drive you there?"

She cringed, but the practical army side came to the forefront. "Thank you."

He nodded. "Let me get my keys from the house."

She watched him lope away, knowing her anxiety had been right on the mark. She needed to be here.

He quickly reappeared and jerked open his passenger-side door. Slowly she approached, eyeing that step up to the cab of his truck. It looked twenty feet higher than her lower-sitting jeep. When she turned to him, he held out his hand. Obviously, he knew her dilemma and his solution solved the problem. She rested her hand on his forearm, noting the tingle was still there, but ignored it and used his arm as a lever to get in.

When he hopped in and started the engine, his presence seemed to dominate the cab of the truck.

Kaye tried to discreetly rub her aching right calf. "How did you know who I was?"

"I've seen your picture at the house. Joel also talks about his sister, the captain."

"Ex-captain."

"Yeah."

"Are you a hired hand at the ranch?" She wanted to avoid explaining why she was an ex-captain.

"No, I'm just a friend who occasionally helps out."

That didn't make a lot of sense. She looked out the window at the familiar sights of home, but somehow the guy sitting beside her managed to make her more aware of him than the scenery. She closed her eyes for a moment, the long day catching up with her.

"We're here."

The words jerked Kaye awake. She glanced around, seeing the emergency entrance of the hospital. Caleb raced around his truck and opened her door. Well, so much for being 100 percent.

Ignoring her embarrassment, she took his hand and got out. Again, her legs didn't cooperate and she fell into him.

He steadied her.

"Thanks."

He didn't make a fuss. "I'll go park the truck."

Watching him drive off, Kaye wished she had the cane that was stuffed in her jeep, but her brain had short-circuited there at the ranch. She took an unsteady step to the emergency room entrance, praying her legs held.

By the time she got to the door, Caleb was there beside her, offering his arm. The instant they walked through the doors the antiseptic smell enveloped her, bringing back memories of the months she spent in various hospitals. Her first instinct was to turn around and walk out.

She must've hesitated because Caleb looked at her. "Are you all right?"

"Yes," she forced out through gritted teeth and walked to the information desk. The grandmotherly lady looked up. "May I help you?"

"My grandfather was brought here. I want to know what his condition is."

"What is his name?"

Before Kaye could answer, she heard, "Sis?"

She turned and saw her brother and grandfather. Gramps was in a wheelchair, an attendant pushing him.

Gramps's right arm was in a sling, and his face sported bruises around his right eye, along with a cut above his brow. His ear looked like one of the cows in the back pasture had been chewing on it or his old, mean bull had stomped him.

"Gramps, are you all right?" She made her way to his side. Fighting her welling emotion, she carefully brushed a kiss across his cheek. When she pulled back, she had to blink away the tears.

"I look worse for wear, but nothing broken," he muttered.

Not trusting her voice, she nodded.

"His shoulder was dislocated," her brother explained.

"They knocked me out before they put the shoulder back in place," Gramps grumbled. "Thought I was too old to stand up to the pain."

Joel fought a grin and managed not to smile.

"I dislocated my shoulder once, Grandpa Niall," Caleb offered. "They didn't knock me out, but the pain did. Be grateful they put you to sleep."

Gramps frowned.

Kaye glanced at Caleb. Nice of him to ease her grandfather's pride. Joel glanced from Caleb to her. She saw the question in her brother's eyes.

"Let's get you home," Kaye said, ignoring her brother.

"I'll go get the truck." Joel raced out of the E.R. Caleb followed.

Gramps looked at her. "What are you doing here?"

"It's good to see you, too."

He waved away the comment. "You know what I mean. You haven't shown up unannounced since the day you graduated from high school and left for the army."

The rebuke hurt, but it was well deserved. "Gramps, I woke up early, and I knew inside I had to come home.

Grandma would've said The Spirit whispered to me." She knew her grandfather would understand her feeling.

"About time."

Leaning down, she whispered, "I'm a little unsteady on my feet after that long drive, so I might need to hold on to your wheelchair."

Glancing up again, his gaze softened.

Both trucks pulled up. Caleb helped her back into his truck while Joel and the attendant got Gramps settled into the front seat of Joel's truck.

"I'll follow behind you," Caleb called out. Getting into his truck, he looked at her. "Seat belt."

"Are you usually so bossy?" Kaye wasn't used to taking orders from civilians.

"No, just safety conscious."

The way he said it made her realize there was more to the situation than just buckling a seat belt. She wondered what.

Caleb glanced over at Kaye. He wasn't surprised exhaustion had overwhelmed her on the drive into Fort Worth. It would've been easier if she'd waited at the ranch, but she'd made it clear she wanted to see her grandfather. Faced with her determination, he couldn't let her drive that last leg herself.

He knew who she was and what had happened to her. When he spent time at the ranch, he stayed in her room. Over the past few years he felt he'd come to know the teenage Brenda. He wasn't sure about this mature woman. Through the countless times he'd stayed there, she'd crept into his consciousness. Seeing her this afternoon in person had knocked him for a loop.

The sparks of attraction he felt dumbfounded him. He was at the ranch to sort out the mess his life had become.

His reaction was the last thing he expected. At least that was what he told himself.

"I'm glad Gramps only had his shoulder dislocated. When I saw him under that tractor, I had all sorts of visions. Once he started yelling at me, I could breathe again. It surely was a sweet sound."

"Thanks for helping him."

"Anyone would've done that."

"No, they wouldn't."

The force of her words made him realize her comment came from experience.

She studied him before asking, "You said you were a friend of my brother's from his rodeo days."

"That's where we met."

"That was a while ago, wasn't it?"

"Ouch, I'm not that old," he teased.

"I've been gone that long."

"Can't be that long ago, since you're still a young woman."

She threw him a look that said she didn't buy his line. "Remember, I've dealt with a lot of males in the army who tried to snow me."

"I call 'em as I see 'em."

Her gaze jerked back to his. She searched his face as if looking for the truth, then turned to stare out her window.

He wanted to ask more questions, but from her closed posture, he knew she wouldn't welcome any. Instead, he turned on the radio to fill the silence on the balance of the ride back to the ranch.

An hour later, he pulled his truck next to Joel's by the back door. Joel helped Gramps from his truck. By the time Kaye unhooked her belt, Caleb had opened the passenger door. She didn't hesitate this time but stepped down to the ground. Her legs were steadier.

They followed Gramps up the porch steps and into the kitchen. Sweat beaded on his forehead. "I think I'll lie down for a while."

Joel walked Gramps to the master bedroom, which was Joel's parents' old room. Kaye settled at the kitchen table, her face fixed on the disappearing figures.

Caleb joined her. "Your grandfather is quite something. Nothing seems to stop him."

"He's amazing, for sure."

Joel appeared and joined them.

Resting her elbows on the table, Kaye asked, "How is Gramps, really?"

Joel wiped his hand over his face. "The doctors and nurses in the E.R. were amazed that only his arm was dislocated. I told them he was a tough old coot." Joel rested his hand over hers. "I'm glad you're here, Sis, but what prompted you to come home now? Don't get me wrong, you're welcome, but—"

"What is this? First Gramps, then you. I'm beginning to feel unwelcome."

Joel wrapped his arm around his sister and hugged her. "It's a surprise, but a happy one." He fell silent. The truth wasn't pretty. "Obviously, you've met Caleb."

"He introduced himself. He knew me, but I—"

"She wondered who I was," Caleb explained, "and where you and your grandfather were. She wasn't too thrilled finding a stranger here who knew her name. For a minute there, I thought she might take me down."

Joel's lips twisted into a smile. "I don't know how much Caleb said about himself, but we were friends when I was on the circuit. He comes here occasionally and visits."

"So that fancy horse trailer I saw outside isn't yours, but Caleb's?"

"It is."

Kaye turned to Caleb. "So what's your specialty in rodeo?"

Caleb's expression closed down. "I'll grab my things and clear out of Kaye's room."

He didn't wait to hear their response but strode into Kaye's room and gathered the two shirts and jeans hanging in the closet. Snagging his duffel bag, he slung it over his shoulder. He looked around the room. Obviously, her family hadn't touched anything in here since Kaye left. An old, faded poster from a Petra concert hung on the wall, along with posters for a world-championship rodeo. Dried mums from her high school homecoming and pom-poms hung over the dresser mirror. Yearbooks sat on the nightstand with a stuffed bear perched on top of them. When Caleb had first stayed in this room, he felt odd. But as time passed, it was like coming back and talking to a friend.

When he turned to go, Kaye stood in the door, her duffel bag and backpack slung over her shoulders, staring at him. Joel stood behind her. He felt four times an idiot to be caught mooning after his abrupt retreat from the kitchen. She must wonder at his actions, but she'd blindsided him with her question.

"I think I've got everything," he said, looking around, giving himself time to take a deep breath. When he turned back, he realized there was no way that he could go through the doorway with his things and not press up against Kaye. He backed up, allowing Kaye and Joel into the room.

She put her duffel bag on the bed and brushed back one of the short brown curls that fell on her forehead. "It always stays the same, doesn't it?" She pointed to the mums. "I guess I need to do some updating."

Joel put down another duffel bag. "Yeah, I don't know why you saved Kenny James's mums."

"Spoken like a brother. Kenny was fun and he asked me to homecoming my senior year."

Joel rolled his eyes and looked at Caleb.

"It's something a girl does." Caleb remembered the corsage his mother had kept from her wedding before a judge.

"What's Kenny doing now?" Kaye slipped off her backpack and put it on the bed beside the duffel bag.

Joel shrugged. "His sister claims he's some bigwig back East. I don't know if that's the truth, but he sure was a bust in rodeo." Joel grinned at Caleb. "The guy flew off the horse the instant the gate opened. He missed his calf in the calf roping, and when he saw the bull he'd pulled to ride, he withdrew."

"Some guys aren't cut out to rodeo." Kaye waved her brother away.

Her words struck a chord in Caleb's heart, making his doubts roar back to life. He took a deep breath.

"Now, get out of here and let me unpack. I think I'd like to take a shower."

As Caleb walked out of the room, he heard brother and sister teasing each other. The banter made him smile, reminding him of the exchanges he had with his younger brother, Sawyer. Now that Sawyer had his degree and no longer needed Caleb's help, there was no reason for Caleb to continue working in the rodeo.

Lately, he'd been dreaming of his own ranch and wondered if that distraction caused the disaster or at least contributed to the accident.

Opening the side door to the horse trailer, Caleb hung his clothes and put his duffel bag on the bunk. He walked out to the corral behind the barn. His horse, Razor, trotted up to him, looking for a treat.

"Sorry, big guy. I don't have anything."

The horse nudged him. Razor could always be depended

on to bring him out of his funk. "Did you see her? Kaye is home. I'd only seen pictures of her, but meeting her in person—wow." Absently, he rubbed Razor's nose as he thought of those blue eyes, which could bore through a man. You weren't going to hide anything from her.

Too bad he hadn't met her before Albuquerque.

Razor lifted his head and galloped around the fence. It brought a smile to Caleb's face.

"I see your horse is in high spirits." Joel stopped beside Caleb.

Caleb rested his booted foot on the bottom rail of the fence. "How's your grandfather, really?"

"Doc says he should be fine. They want him to keep his arm in a sling for the next few days, but nothing was broken. Badly bruised, but not broken. How that tractor didn't do more damage than it did, I don't know. God was looking out for Gramps." Joel kept his gaze on Razor.

"That's for sure. I'm glad I rode out to that pasture." Caleb still remembered the numbing fear that had raced through him when he'd seen the overturned tractor.

"I'm thankful, too."

They both kept their cell phones in their back pockets, and it had proved to be a blessing. Caleb had called and Joel had come within ten minutes.

A deep sigh escaped Joel's mouth. "It's been a day of surprises."

An understatement. "Did you know your sister was coming?"

"Not a clue. I talked with her last week, and she mentioned she was feeling stronger but didn't say anything about coming home. The equine therapy has helped. First time I saw her in the hospital in San Antonio after she'd been wounded, it shook me, and that was weeks after the explosion. It gets to a guy's gut to see his little sister so broken." He looked down at his clasped hands and took a deep breath. "Seeing her now, it's mind-blowing."

"And she's home."

Joel laughed. "Yeah. I often wondered what she was going to do after the army, if she would come home."

"You have part of the question answered." Which was more than Caleb knew about his own life. "Are you glad she's here?"

"Of course, but I'm not sure if she sees it that way. She was good at what she did. The career she loved is over thanks to a suicide bomber, and she comes home to find—" he swept his arm in a wide arc "—this mess with Gramps and the drought. Not to mention she doesn't even know yet about the charity rodeo that I somehow got appointed the head honcho." He blew out a breath and rubbed the back of his neck. "How that happened, I still don't know. This is just one more thing to add confusion to her world. And my world."

They watched Razor.

An idea popped into his brain. "I think I know something that can keep your sister busy and might help her decide what she wants to do." Caleb wanted to laugh out loud at his great idea.

"Yeah, what's that?"

"Put her in charge of the charity rodeo. Let her organize it. You've been complaining constantly about all the things you have to do since you drafted me into this shindig. I thought you were going to drop like a sack of feed when you saw Nan White on the organizing committee."

Joel shuddered. "Who would've thought?"

Anyone with eyes, but Caleb decided not to mention it. "I think with all the different things you and I need to do, giving it to Kaye would keep her busy and she could think of the future."

Joel's distressed expression turned into a grin. "I like how you think, friend."

"Do you think she'll accept?"

Joel shrugged. "Don't know. But I'm going to give it a shot, because heaven knows I don't want to ramrod it."

Caleb shared his friend's feelings about being in charge, but with Kaye running the show, their prospects looked mighty good. And oddly enough, the idea of working with Kaye appealed to him in ways that he didn't understand.

Chapter Two

"Who knew you could cook?" Kaye teased, loading the dishwasher. She leaned against the counter, and her fingers snagged the top wire shelf of the appliance. "And you have a dishwasher—a brand-spanking-new dishwasher." It boggled the mind. Nothing else in this room had changed for over twenty years but this happy little appliance.

Joel leaned back in his chair and grinned. Caleb grabbed his glass of tea and gulped, but she saw his smile.

"A Crock-Pot."

Joel's response didn't make sense. She'd been talking dishwasher. "What?"

"That's my secret to cooking. Once Gramps and I discovered it in the back of the cabinet, we started using it. We had dinner ready when we came in at night." His voice rang with pride.

"It prevented us from starving, that's for sure," Gramps added. The bruising on his face had colored even more, making Kaye want to grimace, remembering when her face had sported similar bruising.

"Well, you'll have to give me some recipes. It's been a long time since I've cooked for myself or my ex—" she swallowed the rest of the bitter word, glancing at Caleb to see if he caught her mistake "—on a regular basis. I think I'd rather be out in the field working with the locals than cook. I guess I didn't get the cooking gene from Mom." She wanted to snatch back the words. How was she going to do this when she kept stepping on land mines?

"Do you have any idea what you want to do now, Sis?" Her brother's question snapped her out of the past.

"You mean, what do I want to do when I grow up?"

That brought laughter.

"Well, I haven't—"

"I have an idea," Joel said.

That had a suspicious ring. She glanced at her grandfather, then Caleb. There was a twinkle in Caleb's eyes that set her teeth on edge. She couldn't tell if Gramps was smiling since his face was so swollen.

"I'm afraid to ask."

Joel stood. "Come with me and I'll show you." He led everyone into the formal dining room. Scattered papers covered the entire surface of the table. "I'm in over my head, and I think with what you did in the army, you can help me."

"At what?" She stared at the mess. It looked like her brother had left the windows open in the dining room and the wind had scattered everything. Stepping to the table, she picked up several sheets. Calf tie-down, steer wrestling, saddle bronc riding, bull riding, bareback riding. "A rodeo?" She looked at the three men gathered around.

"The drought has hit most of the ranchers hard in the county, Sis, nearly wiping us out," Joel explained. "We've had to buy feed and hay since our crops failed. Some don't have the money for seed to plant this next season and will go broke with another year like last year and lose their ranches. At church, we came up with the idea of a charity rodeo with all the prize money, entry fees and ticket sales going to buy seed and feed for the ranchers. County fairgrounds will donate their facility without charge. Now all we have to do is organize the thing." He ran his hand through his hair. "I was elected to organize this shindig and get it going."

Kaye's eyes widened but she didn't say anything. There was more coming, and she felt it.

"I'm in over my head. I can't work the ranch and do this." He waved at the pile. "I could use some help."

There it was.

"Isn't that what you did in the army as a public-affairs officer?" Joel further pressed. "Organizing things for the army and local residents?"

She admired her brother's cunning. He knew how to bait the trap and spring it. When they were growing up, he'd always managed to steer her into doing things he didn't want to do. "You haven't lost your edge, have you, big brother?"

The twitch of his lips ruined his innocent expression.

She tried to remain stern, but the humor of the situation bubbled up. Caleb and Gramps stood still, afraid to breathe. "You were always too smart for my own good."

"Does that mean yes?" The note of hope in her brother's voice made her want to either laugh or throw something at him.

"I'll do it, but you're not off scot-free."

Joel grabbed her around the waist, lifting her off her feet and twirling her around. "That's okay."

"Put me down."

He did, then kissed her on the cheek. "Thanks, Sis."

Kaye shook her head. "What more could I expect from my big brother, who was known to get his own way?" She also figured she needed to pay him back. He'd kept the ranch running when she'd run so fast away from here, leaving him to pick up the pieces.

"Want to see what I've got so far?"

"No, but if I'm going to do this, I guess I need to see what I'm up against. Show me."

Caleb stood by the corral, watching Razor. The spring night carried soft smells of honeysuckle and wild roses. In spite of the drought, some flowers were blooming this year.

There was the hope of rain this week. A promise. Every rancher in the county prayed rain would come.

"Is that your horse?"

Caleb jerked at the sound of Kaye's voice.

"Yes. That's Razor."

"He's a beaut."

Razor trotted up to the fence. He stood before Kaye, his tail swishing.

She reached out her hand to rub the horse's muzzle.

"I wouldn't do that." Caleb's hand shot out catching her by the wrist. The contact sizzled. Her eyes widened as she felt the electricity, too. Instantly, he drew back his hand. "He's prickly."

Kaye turned her gaze back to Razor and lightly stroked the horse's muzzle and forehead. Amazingly, stunningly, Razor stood quietly and allowed her to do it, making him look like an idiot.

"*This* is prickly?" She moved her hand under his chin and continued stroking him. "Hey, big guy. It's nice to meet you." She reached into the pocket of her light sweater and pulled out a carrot. "Could I offer you a treat?"

Razor nodded and closed his teeth around the carrot.

Leaning against the fence, Caleb marveled at the woman's approach. "You came prepared."

"I learned the hard way it's always easier to offer a gift. It paves the way. It works with people as well as animals. Particularly in Iraq."

Joel had bragged about what his sister did in the army. And Caleb had stayed at the ranch the week Joel and his grandfather had visited her in the hospital in San Antonio.

"Razor is the best at what he does, but some folks have gotten on the wrong side of him." Caleb felt foolish for sounding the alarm, but who knew Razor would behave himself? "Razor is a fine working horse, but he's a little temperamental."

"Temperamental?"

"Folks need to be cautious when they approach him. He can be unpredictable. He needs a firm hand."

"I understand. I've spent the last twelve years dealing with prickly males."

Caleb's eyes widened, then he snorted. "Point taken." He liked her quick wit.

"Well, he's a beautiful animal. And I think I've won a friend."

"Just be warned, he'll be looking for a treat from now on."

"I hear you. But remember, I was a public-affairs officer. My job was to read people and interface with the local population."

"Interface?"

She caught the irony in his voice. "Sorry. Force of habit. It's easier to talk and get to know the local civilian population if you come with a present." She sobered. "I guess I've joined the ranks of that civilian population, haven't I?"

Obviously, the lady's choice hadn't been one she'd welcomed. Circumstances had overwhelmed her. He identified with that. "But something tells me you're the right person to tackle that charity rodeo. Since you *interfaced* with the locals, I think you can probably do this job in your sleep."

"Sometimes dealing with your own hometown is more of a challenge."

He knew that. "You'll be better than Joel. Or me."

She laughed, a clear, beautiful sound that transformed her into a stunning woman. He didn't think she had on a speck of makeup, but there was a natural beauty to her. She wasn't like some of those girls who showed up at the rodeo, playing at being a cowgirl, pretending to be something they weren't. He could tell that Kaye had been through some hard experiences, but she wore that experience with dignity. And *that* appealed to him.

"Well, since I'm at a crossroads, I guess I've got the time." Razor dipped his head, looking for another carrot. She gently pushed his face away. "One wasn't enough for you?"

The horse raised his head. She pulled a second carrot out of her other pocket. The horse nodded and took the second one from her. "If I pull this thing off, are you going to compete?"

"Not me."

"Why not? I though you said you knew Joel through the rodeo."

"True, but that was a long time ago. I started working as a pick-up rider. My brother was the star."

"Oh, good, you could ride pick-up for the charity rodeo. That will work, as well."

"No can do." He didn't look at her but rubbed Razor's neck.

"Why not?"

She'd touched a raw spot in his heart. He didn't know if he wanted to charge that hill yet, so he hoped to divert her. "I can help with other things—with your vendors, stock supplier, but I won't do pick-up."

Confusion filled her eyes, and she opened her mouth, but then closed it. "Okay. I'll take you up on the offer to help."

He nodded.

She studied him. "If you don't mind me asking, why'd you become a pick-up rider? Most of the guys I knew growing up here wanted to compete and win. That's where the action and glory are."

"And if they don't win or place, they don't get money. What I did pays every rodeo." And since he'd supported his brother and him, he'd needed a paycheck he could count on. He knew she wanted to ask more, but he wasn't willing to say more. "Why'd you join the army?"

"At the time, it seemed the best choice." Her bleak tone told the story.

He'd sung that same song, the same verse of that heart-wrenching tune. Of course, he knew the real reason she'd joined the army. He'd been with Joel in Phoenix getting ready for the rodeo when Joel had gotten the bad news his parents and grandmother had been killed in a car accident. That New Year's Eve had dramatically changed his friend's life. Kaye's, too.

He stole a glance at her. Her expression told him she didn't want to talk anymore about why she'd joined the army.

"You must've liked the army since you became a captain."

Facing him, she leaned against the fence. "You know the thing I liked the most about the army?"

"What was that?"

"The order. And structure. You can depend on certain things. And you always knew that you'd have a place to sleep, clothes on your back and three squares a day."

He understood that. There were times when he hadn't known where Sawyer and he would get their next meal. They'd often did without when they were living with his mother, but once he'd had custody of his brother, they'd never gone without. "I understand."

His tone must've caught her ear, because her gaze searched his. "You do?"

"Yup, I had more peanut-butter-and-sugar sandwiches and ramen noodles than I care to think about."

Razor bumped her shoulder. "Sorry, big guy, you ate it all." She rubbed his nose. "I'll come prepared with more next time." Razor nodded.

"I think you're on his good side."

"I'm glad I haven't completely lost my touch, unlike my stumbling into this rodeo deal. Joel may have thought he pulled one on me, but I'm not going to let you and my brother off the hook. I'll need help." Her tone brooked no argument.

He raised his hands. "I told you I'd help."

She nodded. "This rodeo is scheduled for the last weekend of May. That gives me ten weeks. I've done events for the army in less time, but I had the manpower."

"Which means that you're going to be working us hard."

"You got it, cowboy." The humor in her eyes matched the curve of her lips. "Will you be available? You don't have a rodeo scheduled, do you?"

Her consideration astonished and sobered him. He knew if he called Steve Carter now, he could be working next week. She hadn't assumed. She'd thought to ask. At her rank, issuing orders was natural. His respect for her grew. "I've got the time, and between you and Joel, I think you'll keep me busy."

"Thanks, Caleb." She turned and walked toward the house. He saw that she limped noticeably. When she got to the stairs, she paused, then slowly placed her right foot on the first step. She brought her left foot up to the riser before she tackled the next one. He knew she'd broken both legs in several places, but never once today had she complained.

Razor nudged him with his nose.

"Well, you made me look like an idiot. Here I was issuing a warning about what a skittish creature you are." Razor moved his head, wanting his chin scratched. "Then you rolled over for her like a big puppy. I bet Bart McQueen would be amazed." Bart had a nasty bruise on his thigh thanks to Razor.

Razor picked his head up and nodded.

"Traitor," he grumbled as he walked to his trailer. Shucking off his boots, he stretched out on the bunk. Folding his arms behind his head, he remembered Kaye's struggle up the steps.

The lady had guts. And smarts. And he didn't doubt she was going to run Joel and him to the ground.

Oddly, he didn't mind.

Kaye reread the verse Ps 94:17. *Unless the Lord had been my help, my soul had almost dwelt in silence.* She closed her Bible and felt the deep peace that scripture brought her. She remembered waking up in the hospital in Ramstein, Germany hearing that verse. She'd been in and out of consciousness, and when she'd finally awoken, night nurse 2nd Lt. Jenna Mayfield had been there, reading to her from the Bible.

Each time Kaye read that verse, she knew that God had shielded her. "I don't know what I'm to do now, Lord. Why'd you save me and not the others?" She'd been meeting a group of Iraqi women, talking to them, seeing what they needed and how the U.S. Army could help them. They'd made progress. After nearly four months, the women had trusted her enough to tell her of the dreams they had for their children. They'd been excited about the

opening of a new school, and even girls were being edu-
cated. They'd been friends. She recalled clearly each face
and the hope and excitement.

She took a long steadying breath as the sorrow washed
over her. None of the five women had made it. The only
reason Kaye had survived was because when the bomb
went off she'd been reaching down to pick up her backpack to get the small gifts she had for their children. After
the incident, Kaye knew none of the other women in the
neighborhood would talk or cooperate with the Ameri-
cans. She carried the weight of that guilt. That was the
main reason she resigned.

The light knock on the door caught her by surprise.
"Sis?"

"Come in, Joel."

He cracked the door. "I wanted to say thanks again for
doing this." He walked into the room and sat on the edge
of the bed beside her. "When I saw you standing there in
the emergency room, it seemed like an answer to prayer.
I didn't know how I was going to manage Gramps, the
ranch and this rodeo at the same time."

"Caleb was here."

Joel's eyes widened. "He's a guy."

She cocked her head. "So?"

"Guys aren't as good as girls at taking care of sick
folks."

"Please, Joel. I've been watching men do the cooking
and cleaning and nursing for the past twelve years."

"Okay." He raised his hands. "But you are an answer
to prayer. I'm glad you're home, Sis."

Was she an answer to prayer? Hardly, but was this rodeo
an answer to prayer? "I'm glad I'm home, too, and Gramps
is okay."

"You're planning on staying, aren't you?"

"I don't know, Joel. I know this is where I should be now. Helping with the rodeo might help me to know what my next step is."

Joel slipped his arm around her shoulders and hugged her. "My mind went on overload when Caleb called this morning. I honestly don't know how we moved the tractor, but we did." He rubbed his neck. "I hope you don't mind that Caleb's here and spent time at the ranch."

"Why would I mind? I haven't lived here in a long time."

"You still own half of this ranch."

"If you want to be technical, yes, but really, this place is yours. You're the guy who put his sweat and blood into it and oversaw everything since Mom and Dad died. You and Gramps."

He nodded. "I'm glad you feel that way. Welcome home, Sis." He kissed her cheek and walked out of the room.

Turning off the light, she slipped between the sheets. Home. She was really home. The house hadn't changed much since she'd left, kind of like it was in a male time warp. The only thing new was the sixty-inch TV that took over half the wall in the living room. And that dishwasher. The house sported a twenty-year-old stove, a toaster that belonged to her grandmother, a washer and dryer her mother had bought the year Kaye was born. But that brand-spanking-new TV had all the bells and whistles on it and sported the football and rodeo channels.

Men were so predictable.

And when she'd walked into her bedroom earlier today, there had stood Caleb among all the tokens that the teenage Brenda had thought were important. It had rattled her and touched part of her soul she buried with her divorce. Here was a handsome man who saw her as a woman. Not Captain Kaye, meal-ticket Kaye or poor, pitiful Brenda who'd lost her parents.

Joel may have thought he'd put one over on her by dumping this rodeo in her lap, but she welcomed it. She'd been restless these past few weeks as she finished her equine therapy. Being around horses had put a longing in her heart to go home. But she'd known if she went home, she'd have to make peace with the past she'd successfully avoided until now. The thought frightened her. But maybe working on the rodeo would keep her busy enough to deal with the past or ignore it, which she preferred. And maybe she'd find the road God wanted her to walk for the rest of her life.

Maybe.

Chapter Three

"Yes, Nan, I'll be in contact. And rest assured Joel definitely isn't getting off scot-free," Kaye added, getting up from the formal dining room table. One of the house phones had a cordless handset.

"Well, I hope so. I volunteered only because Joel asked. Don't get me wrong. I would've helped with the rodeo," Nan hastily added, "but not as one of the board members with all the extra work it requires. But the local ranchers need the help."

"I will talk to Joel and the other two board members. Why don't we meet this Saturday morning? Is the Country Kitchen Café downtown still there and in business?"

"Yes, it is."

"Good. Then let's meet there and coordinate what needs to be done. If we need to look at the fairgrounds, we can."

"All right. You'll notify the others?"

"I will." Kaye disconnected and set the phone on the table, taking a deep breath.

She'd spent the morning going over the papers scattered across the formal dining room table, putting them in some sort of order. It reminded her of some of the offices in Baghdad. She'd spent the morning writing a list of things that needed to be done. More than once she'd wanted to throw up her hands and walk away from the mess. But as soon as that thought had occurred, the army side of her came roaring back, determined to make order out of the chaos. The ranchers needed the money, and the rodeo would raise those funds.

"How did you let your brother hornswoggle you into doing his job?"

Looking up, she spied her grandfather at the door. "Good question. I must be off my game."

Gramps walked slowly to the table. When he sat, he adjusted the sling holding his right arm. "I think I'm going to throw this contraption into the trash."

Standing, she came to his side. "Here, let me do that. You want it looser or tighter?"

"I want it gone."

Apparently, she was going to pull rank on the old boy. "That's fine, but I'm sure the doctors told you that it would take longer for that shoulder to recover without it. And if you want to mess with this longer, then ignore the medical advice. I know how annoying it is, because there in San Antonio I refused therapy until one drill sergeant of a head nurse told me to move my sorry bu—posterior out of her ward. She only wanted those patients who were brave enough to heal. I had to do a lot of things I didn't want to do these past six months to be able to walk again."

His mouth compressed into a frown. "Going to use guilt on me, are you, girl?"

"If it works, I'm using it."

She could see her grandfather considering her words. "I like how the army trained you."

"If I was still in the army, I'd simply give you an order."

He laughed. "I bet you were a handful."

"According to Mom, I always was a handful." The mention of her mom sobered her.

Gramps rested his hand on her arm. "You need to make peace with what happened."

She tried not to jerk away, but his words were like a live wire touching her skin. "What about your sling?"

"I need this thing looser."

She readjusted the strap.

"So can you make sense of this mess?" He nodded toward the table that now sported neat stacks of papers.

"Barely. I've been looking through everything. What I need is Joel in here, not outside chasing down cows."

"Why not call the other folks on the committee?"

"I just finished talking to Nan White. And she told me about Mike Johnson and Laurie Benson."

"I've heard your brother talking to them."

"So why didn't he tell me about the others? I found a note buried in this chaos." Kaye finished adjusting the sling.

"Because Nan recently got divorced and has been eyeballing your brother like he's a side of beef."

A chuckle burst out of her mouth. "So it wasn't my talent that impressed my brother. He just wanted a stand-in."

Gramps started to shrug, but the pain stopped him. He hissed. "I think I might take one of those little pills the hospital gave me and sit in my chair."

"Let's get you settled, then I'll get your meds." She'd been through enough pain; she could identify with Gramps in a way she would've never understood before.

Gramps hobbled into the living room and eased into his well-worn recliner. Kaye grabbed the pills and a glass of water from the kitchen and returned to his side.

He took the meds without any argument, which meant he was hurting. He settled back in the chair and closed his eyes. "Turn on that TV to one of the sports channels and I'll sit here and listen to it."

Kaye smiled and turned on the TV.

"Why don't you go and see if you can corner your brother and drag some answers out of him. I won't move."

Not sure she wanted to leave Gramps, she stood there.

Gramps opened one eye. "Go. Midnight is out in the corral."

She didn't want to insult her grandfather, so she retrieved the handset from the dining room table and put it on the table beside the chair. "I've put the phone by your chair. Call if you need anything."

He nodded and waved her away.

She kissed Gramps's forehead and reluctantly walked away, praying she'd made the right decision.

Out on the back porch, she stretched her protesting back and shoulders. Sitting that long had allowed her muscles to stiffen, and she'd worked so hard to build them up. The first time she'd gotten out of the hospital bed in San Antonio, she'd landed on her backside, her muscles like jelly. She'd done it in front of the drill-sergeant nurse, but that weakness made her realize she needed to fight.

Midnight was in the corral behind the barn, as Gramps had said. A ride just might be the thing. Besides, after talking to Nan and Gramps, she had a few things she wanted to discuss with her brother.

Nan had been great after Kaye had told her what her job in the army had been. Kaye planned to talk to the other two members of the committee later, after she "chatted" with her brother. He was still the head honcho and she needed his input.

Stopping before the fence, Kaye called out to the horse. "Midnight, want a peppermint?" She held up the treat and noisily unwrapped it. The horse trotted to her side, putting her face near Kaye's hands. "Oh, you're easy. Didn't take much convincing, did it?" The horse happily lipped the candy. Kaye slipped the bridle over the horse's head and walked her into the barn. It only took moments for Kaye to saddle the mare. Kaye found the wooden folding steps they kept in the corner of the barn and used them to mount the horse. She looked forward to the day she wouldn't need the extra help with mounting. Before the accident, she could pull herself into the saddle with ease.

She shook off the pity party. There was no use in playing the what-if game.

Touching her back pocket, Kaye made sure she had her cell phone. She considered calling Joel, but she wanted to surprise him with questions about the rodeo and didn't want to give him time to come up with an excuse.

She studied the western horizon, noting the gathering clouds. "It looks like we might get some rain," she told Midnight, patting the horse on her neck. "We can only pray it does." She guided Midnight back inside the barn and snagged her old cowboy hat from a hook. It amazed her that her brother had kept it, but she'd put it to good use.

"Let's see if we can find the guys before we have some weather." She remembered they'd talked about checking the stock at the western edge of the ranch.

As she rode away from the barn, she felt a freedom, and long-ago hopes flickered to life in her heart, sparking a smile. The years seemed to melt away and she didn't have a care in the world.

Her body relaxed into the rhythm of the horse's gait. When she was in the army, she'd always found a stable where she was stationed so she could ride, but riding here at her family's ranch brought back good memories. The wind picked up and the sky grew dark. After several minutes, when she still hadn't seen any signs of either Joel or

Caleb, she considered going back to the ranch house. The land dipped toward a small stream. Trees grew in abundance down here by the river, and it was always a place where they had to rescue stray calves. Maybe she'd find the guys there.

As she headed toward the stream, a blinding light split the sky, and the ground shook with the earth-shattering sound. Her mount danced sideways and electricity seemed to race over Kaye's skin, raising the hair on her arms. She struggled with the reins, trying to keep the horse from bolting.

"Easy, girl."

The horse's head came up and Midnight shook. Kaye patted the mare's neck. "Easy." What she didn't need was her mount charging off in a blind panic.

As she nudged her horse forward, she thought she heard her name, turned and saw Caleb racing toward her.

Before he could reach her, the sky opened up as if someone had turned on the shower full throttle. These were no little droplets but a full barrage of stinging drops.

"Let's take cover under the trees," he shouted, nodding toward the stand of trees.

They both headed for the shelter. They were almost there when another flash of lightning streaked across the sky. The boom nearly threw Kaye off her horse, singeing her skin and throwing her back to another blast that tore her world apart.

"Wow, that was close." Caleb looked around to make sure the lightning hadn't hit any of the trees surrounding them. When Kaye didn't answer, he turned to her. They were both drenched and the cold rain ran down his back in rivulets. But what chilled him was Kaye's blank expression.

"Kaye, were you hit?"

Kaye appeared frozen.

He nudged his horse closer to her. "Are you hurt?" He did a quick scan for any injuries.

Again, she didn't answer.

"Kaye, are you okay?"

Her eyes were wide-open, but she wasn't seeing him next to her. She clutched her horse's reins so tightly that her fingers had gone white. Her mount danced nervously. Caleb reached over and pried her fingers loose from the reins. Her body began to shake so hard, he thought she'd fly apart. And she wasn't doing her mount any favors.

"Kaye?"

Nothing.

Another flash of lightning, accompanied by booming thunder filled the air. Kaye seemed to shrink farther into herself.

Caleb grabbed Midnight's reins and wrapped them around his saddle horn, then pulled Kaye from her saddle and settled her in front of him. He took off her cowboy hat and folded her close to his chest.

Her body shook as if she were on a Tilt-a-Whirl at the state fair. He rested his chin on her head and rubbed his hand over her back. The world around them disappeared while Caleb held this brave woman, who was seeing another world, living through a different storm.

He could only guess at the horror she saw, but he knew she'd endured a lot in the hospitals she'd been in. He experienced nightmares about the accident that had just happened with the rider who was hurt, but his nightmares were nowhere in the realm of hers.

Midnight danced, but Razor stood rock steady underneath him. Midnight calmed.

Caleb started praying. He might not know what she saw, but God did.

The storm raged around them, cutting them off from the world. The leaves shook, but only a few drops worked their way down Caleb's back. As he prayed, Caleb felt a deep connection to this woman—one he'd never experienced before. He didn't quite understand the feeling, but he recognized a wounded soul when he saw one.

He lost track of how much time passed, but the lack of sound finally caught his attention. The rain stopped as suddenly as it began.

Kaye's body relaxed and she melted into him. He continued to hold her, lightly rubbing her back. After a moment, she stirred and looked up at him.

Slowly she became aware of where she sat. She didn't cry or accuse but quietly waited for an explanation.

"You seemed a bit— Uh, Midnight panicked and—"

She looked down at her hands. "Thanks."

No further explanation was needed.

He wanted to ask her what she was reliving, but from her closed expression, he knew she didn't want to talk.

"I think I can ride by myself." She refused to look up.

"So how do you want to do this? You want to try to slip your leg over Midnight's back, or do you want to mount from the ground?"

She eyed the maneuver she would have to make to slip onto Midnight's back from his horse. "I think maybe let me mount from the ground."

He gently set her on her feet, handed back her hat then unwrapped her mount's reins from around his saddle horn. She slapped the hat on and looked around—he guessed for a rock that she could mount from.

He dismounted and cupped his hands so she could use them for a boost up.

"Thanks."

She stepped into his hands and he lifted her over her horse's back. Her neck turned red.

He remounted his horse and they started toward the house. They didn't talk as they rode, but as they topped the next-to-last rise before the ranch house, the sight and smell of smoke filled the sky.

Kaye stopped. Caleb stopped beside her.

"The house and barn are in that direction." She glanced at him.

"There were several lightning strikes close to us. Maybe one of the trees or some grass burned." At least he hoped that was all it was.

They kicked their mounts into a run. As they topped the last rise, their worst fears were confirmed. The back porch of the house was on fire. Joel and her grandfather fought the flames.

Riding down the hill, they galloped to the barn. Joel stood outside with the hose, and Gramps held a bucket. Caleb raced to the back of the house and dismounted on a run. He took the bucket from the old man and ran to the outside trough and filled it. He threw the bucket on the edge of the porch. Kaye went inside and grabbed the broom and started to beat the two-by-fours anchoring the screens.

They worked for several more minutes at fighting the fire until they had it out. Finally, Joel stepped back and held the hose at his side. "I think we've got it. Anyone see any smoldering spots?"

"Looks like it's out," Caleb said.

Gramps stumbled to the singed picnic table and sat. Caleb set the bucket down. He collapsed next to Gramps on the bench as Joel turned off the hose.

Opening the screen door, Kaye joined the others. Part of the porch's roof was blackened.

"What happened?" she asked.

"I was riding in when I saw the bolt of lightning hit the porch. I vaulted off my horse and ran to the hose and started fighting the flames. Gramps came out the back door and tried to help, but—"

"I was sitting in my chair asleep when a loud crack woke me. What that tractor didn't do, the boom nearly did."

They looked at the smoldering roof of the porch.

"It could've been worse," Caleb said. His words were punctuated by the roof crumbling onto the porch.

Silence settled until a choked laugh escaped Kaye. She looked around, guilt flushing her cheeks.

Joel shook his head. Caleb fought his smile while Gramps just shook his head and walked back inside.

Caleb thought about what Joel said. "Did you see the lightning actually strike the house?"

Under the soot on his face, Joel frowned. "I did. Why?"

"Horsefeathers." Gramps's comment drifted through the screened back door.

Caleb rubbed the back of his neck. "Because if there was a direct strike, it probably fried all the electronics in the house."

Kaye sat down next to Caleb. "What else could go wrong?"

"Do you really want to know?"

She shook her head. "No."

But when it rained, it poured. And it was raining hard.

Chapter Four

Kaye pulled the marshmallow out of the fireplace and placed it onto a graham cracker. She topped it with a square of chocolate and a second graham cracker, and handed it to her grandfather. "This reminds me of the first time you took Joel and me on a campout."

Gramps accepted the treat and tried to take a bite but lost hold of the s'more. It plopped in his lap. He glanced at Kaye. "Nothing's going right today."

Kaye quickly picked up the s'more and put it on a plate. "I'll make you another."

Gramps shook his head. "Nope, just give me back that mess. I'll finish it."

Kaye glanced at Caleb and saw him grinning. A laugh bubbled up in her, but she didn't think Gramps would appreciate it. After the events of this afternoon, you had to either laugh or cry. She put the plate with the s'more in Gramps's lap. He picked it up and took a bite.

Caleb handed her another marshmallow. "You seem to get the marshmallow just right, so mind doing mine?"

Kaye's emotions binged all over the place. There was that sizzle she felt, but also she was on pins and needles, worried he'd ask about what happened during the storm.

This flashback had been the worst she'd experienced.

"Kaye?" Caleb said again, holding out the marshmallow.

"Well, since your last marshmallow resembled the black mess on the back porch, I guess I could."

Caleb grinned. "That last one I did looked exactly like the mess on the porch."

The lightning had blown all the lightbulbs in the house along with all the appliances—big screen included. Even the hot-water heater had been fried. Joel called the insurance company on his cell phone and was told to leave things alone until the adjuster could get out to the ranch tomorrow. If they had any working cameras or if their cell phones had a camera they should take pictures of the damages.

They'd put the things from the refrigerator in an ice chest and had hot dogs for dinner. The fire in the fireplace was Gramps's idea. They had only two lightbulbs in the pantry, so they'd replaced one in Gramps's room but had to find a lamp that still worked to put in the other lightbulb. Luckily, all their flashlights worked.

"I wonder if we're the only ones who got hit," Joel said.

"I'll ask when I call the other members on the committee. Oh, by the way, I talked to Nan today." Kaye pulled the marshmallow out of the fire and handed the skewer to Caleb.

In the light from the fireplace, Kaye could see her brother's guilty look. "Oh?"

"That's why I decided to ride out to the field, to have a little talk with you."

Joel shifted on the chair. "About what?"

"About all the details I couldn't find in your pile. Have you assigned jobs to the various board members? Nan didn't know what she was to do."

In the dim light, Kaye couldn't tell if he blushed, but he wouldn't look at her.

Joel stuffed the last of the s'more in his mouth. "Not exactly," he mumbled around the graham cracker.

Her brother acted more like a teenage boy than an adult male. Caleb and Gramps avoided looking at her, too.

"We're going into town Saturday morning to meet with the other members on the board of the charity rodeo. If we're going to pull this off in the allotted time, everyone needs to be assigned a job, so before I do that, I want to talk to all the board members."

"Well, let me know how it goes." Joel tried to hand her another marshmallow.

"Oh, no, big brother." Her firm tone drew everyone's attention. "You and Caleb are going with me. Remember, you promised to help."

He opened his mouth, then closed it.

She readied herself to bat down any further arguments. "Gramps, if you want to come, you're more than welcome."

Gramps nodded. "Better than sitting here with nothing working."

Kaye took the marshmallow from Joel.

"So why didn't you just call, Sis? When that storm hit, I thought you were here with Gramps."

She paled at the question and her gaze flew to Caleb's. His expression remained neutral. "After talking with Nan, I wanted to get some straight answers from you."

"And you found Caleb, instead."

"I did." Kaye battled the fear that Caleb would mention how she froze up.

"We were caught out there in the field when the lightning struck," Caleb explained. "Nearly rattled all the teeth out of my head and didn't do our horses any favors. We raced toward that copse of trees, took shelter and rode out the storm." Nothing in his tone indicated she'd flipped out.

Joel's eyes narrowed. "I had to fight my mount when one of those strikes hit close."

"As I said, our mounts weren't happy, either." Caleb popped the last of his s'more into his mouth. Was there a pattern here? Stuff the mouth and don't have to answer the question.

Kaye anxiously waited, but Caleb simply continued eating his treat. He nodded toward the bowl of marshmallows.

"Could you do in another one?" he asked between bites.

His question snapped her out of her anxiety. She searched Caleb's gaze and realized he wasn't going to say anything about her flashback. "Sure." She put two marshmallows on a skewer and held it over the flames.

A weight lifted off her shoulders. Still reeling from the incident, she didn't want her family to know about what happened. Flashbacks weren't that unusual for combat veterans and she'd had a few before now, but this last one was a real doozy. The noise of the thunder and sudden change in the air pressure had resembled the moments around when the bomb detonated. She remembered being pushed down into blackness when the bomb had gone off in the café. Snatches of the minutes after the bomb floated through her memory.

The cries.

The moans.

The stickiness of blood on her face.

And the metallic smell of blood and biting smell of cordite.

Through the panic this afternoon, a prayer had pierced the nightmare. The words had been a lifeline in the sea of pain and terror that she'd grabbed on to and held until the nightmare receded. When the world had come back into focus, Caleb's strong arms had surrounded her. He'd smelled of man and wet horse, which had been a blessing and comfort. It was reality that she held on to.

She'd feared Caleb might ask what was wrong, but he hadn't. And he hadn't ratted her out to her brother when he'd had the opportunity.

"I think those marshmallows are ready," Caleb whispered.

Jerking the marshmallows back, she pushed one onto the graham cracker he held.

"Thanks."

Kaye nodded, thinking she was the one who should thank him. She breathed a sigh of relief, and the knot in her stomach eased. Caleb had just won her respect. And gratitude. When she looked at him, there was no disdain in his eyes, simply understanding.

"Whoever would've thought we'd be roasting our dinner over the fireplace," Gramps grumbled. "I remember it wasn't until I was eight before my folks got electricity at their ranch. I liked the convenience."

"Well, tomorrow's going to be a big day. After the insurance man comes, I'm going shopping. If y'all want any input into the purchases, you'd better come with me."

"You can do that, Sis. We've got a lot to do here."

"You know better what appliances we need," Gramps added.

"Fine, but I think we don't need that big a TV again. It seems a bit extreme." That brought both of them up short.

Gramps opened his mouth, but Joel beat him to the punch. "Just do it in the afternoon, Sis. We need to care for the stock."

"Not a problem." Kaye swallowed her grin. Out of the corner of her eye, she saw the mirth in Caleb's face. This wasn't the first time she'd maneuvered around obstinate men.

* * *

Kaye couldn't sleep. Each time she closed her eyes, the smell of burned wood filled her lungs, reminding her of her flashback and the horror of cresting that last hill and seeing her home on fire. Or of a burning café in Baghdad.

She threw back the covers and scrambled out of bed, looking around for her beat-up jeans. She threw off her sleep shirt, slipped on her army-issued T-shirt and her running shoes and headed for the barn. She needed to check on Midnight. They'd both had a tough day.

Slipping out the kitchen door, she noticed that the moon washed the charred remains of the porch in silver light. It didn't look as stark in moonlight, but with daylight the ugly scars would be there again.

She identified with that. She looked okay from the outside, but if you shone sunlight on her, you could see the burned and damaged parts. Her legs were crossed with cuts and burns, and she had massive scars from the surgery.

When she walked into the barn, the warm, comforting scent of horse filled her lungs, replacing the biting, charred smell of wood. She walked down the stalls and stopped at Midnight's. She slipped inside and softly crooned to the horse. Midnight woke and turned to her.

"Sorry, girl, for waking you. I just wanted to make sure you were okay. Obviously, you are." Kaye rubbed the horse's muzzle. The horse snorted and nodded her head. Kaye slipped out of the stall, grabbed a curry brush and went back inside. "I didn't mean to freak out on you." With long strokes she worked the brush over the horse's flank. "This time was… There weren't words for this afternoon."

That fact rattled Kaye. And of course, that memory was joined by other hidden memories lurking in this house. All the joy and laughter of her childhood drowned out by the sorrow that had reigned those last months of high school.

She'd tried to remain numb her last months home, but thoughts of her folks had kept ambushing her. Her mom wasn't there to help her pick out a dress for prom if she'd gone, and her dad didn't get to see her graduate. Grandma never showed her how to make her special Chess pie. They were all gone in an instant.

Her hand stilled on Midnight's side as she tried to catch her breath. "Lord, I'm drowning. I need something to hold on to. What am I going to do?"

She heard Razor in the next stall. She looked at Midnight and whispered, "I wasn't expecting that."

Kaye slipped out of Midnight's stall and walked to Razor's half door. "I don't think you're who God sent, my friend." Putting down the curry brush on the half door, she rubbed the horse's nose.

"I don't know. Razor's a godsend for a lot of cowboys."

Instinct took over and she dropped to a crouch, ready to fight. Caleb stood at the barn's side door. She relaxed, then tensed, wondering how much of her conversation had he heard. Well, she'd just gut her way through. "What are you doing up?"

"I could ask the same." Caleb walked toward her. "I heard someone out here, then Razor moving, so I came to investigate. With all that's happened today, I thought it wise." He had on jeans, a T-shirt and flip-flops. He walked to her side. "You couldn't sleep, either?"

"Yeah."

She needed to thank him for helping her through the storm and not mentioning it to her family. As she searched for the best way to say it, he said, "Things around here haven't been dull. I think there's more excitement than Joel, Gramps or I could've come up with.

"Putting out fires and lifting tractors wasn't something

I imagined doing when I came to spend a little time with Joel and Gramps." His grin punctuated his words.

"Does that mean you're going to desert us?" She tried to force as much lightness as she could into the words, but they sounded desperate to her ears.

His expression lost all humor. "No. I promised you I'd help, and I keep my promises."

Instantly, she knew this man had been let down by someone he trusted and would not break his word.

"Have you changed your mind about working as the pick-up rider?"

"No. But I could recommend someone."

"I'll take you up on that offer." She paused, wanting to find the right words. "Thank you for not saying anything to Joel and Gramps about what happened out there in the storm." She swallowed. "That lightning strike was so much like… I heard the boom and felt that pressure and sizzle and suddenly…"

"You don't have to explain."

Kaye closed her eyes and nodded, shamed by her weakness. And she wasn't ready to talk to anyone about her memories.

Razor butted her shoulder, throwing her off balance. Caleb caught her. She looked up into his face, and for an instant there was that connection again. Their moment was spoiled when Razor butted her once more. The horse's persistence made her smile. "Is he always so contrary?"

"I warned you about him."

She picked up the curry brush, walked into the stall and began brushing him.

Caleb laughed. "You, my friend," he addressed Razor, "know how to manipulate folks."

"No, he's not a manipulator. Razor is honest in what he wants, unlike my ex-husband." The words were out of her mouth before she thought about them. Her loose lips shocked her. Well, she certainly was airing all her dirty laundry today, wasn't she?

Caleb continued to stroke Razor's nose. "You're right. Razor's honest in what he wants and doesn't choose to hurt others to satisfy his own needs."

Ah, he'd been hurt, too.

Kaye continued to brush the horse but refused to look at him again, knowing that they'd both said too much.

After several minutes of silence, she looked up. Caleb was nowhere to be seen. She didn't know how to feel. How was she going to face him tomorrow?

By the time she walked into the kitchen at eight in the morning, Caleb and Joel were long gone. Someone had taken down the old coffeepot that her grandmother used, plugged it in and there was coffee. She'd spent the night fighting different nightmares. Finally, around four o'clock, she started praying and the last thing she remembered was singing "Amazing Grace" in her mind.

"'Bout time you hauled yourself outta bed," Gramps mumbled as he walked into the kitchen. "You army folks get up this late?"

"Good morning to you, too." She brushed a kiss across his purplish cheek. "I'm glad you found Grandma's coffeepot."

His eyes took on a faraway look. "I remember the first time she made coffee in that pot. Your ma was only a teenager." He shook off the sad feeling. "Your brother and Caleb made coffee and peanut-butter sandwiches and left."

The blown toaster sitting beside the coffeepot had belonged to Grandma, too. After pouring herself a cup of coffee, she sat at the table and slowly looked around the kitchen, taking in her mother's stove and refrigerator. The blender and expensive freestanding mixer had thankfully survived since they weren't plugged in. Mom had saved for six months to get that mixer.

Gramps put the bread and peanut butter on the table. "You might as well make yourself a sandwich." He sat down beside her. "You okay, girl?"

Her head snapped up. "Why would you ask?"

Gramps grabbed her hand. "'Cause my face looks better than yours."

She winced and opened her mouth to argue, but she understood what Gramps was saying. "The stove, refrigerator—they were all picked out by Mom and Grandma."

Gramps folded his hand over hers. "They're just things."

"But there's memories," she whispered, her throat closing up.

"True, and to be sure they're good ones, Brenda Lynn, but they are only things. We needed to replace half those things before nature took care of that. You should cherish those memories, girl, but you gotta make peace with them."

His point hit too close to home. She slathered the peanut butter on a piece of bread and took a bite. With her mouth full, she didn't have to respond.

Before Gramps could say more, there was a knock at the front door. She sprang to her feet, eager to leave the conversation, and saw an old schoolmate through the glass in the door. She opened the door. "Bryan?"

"Hey, Brenda. Long time, no see."

She'd gone through all twelve years of school with Bryan Danvers. "It has been a few years. What are you doing here?"

"I'm your insurance agent." He pointed to the embroidered shirt pocket with the name of the insurance company. "You had a lightning strike?" He looked down at his clipboard.

"We did, and all the males in this house are mourning the death of that sixty-inch TV."

He clutched his chest. "Ouch. I can understand their grief. Why don't you show me where this crime occurred?"

So male. "Follow me."

Caleb rode slowly up to the stand of trees where Kaye and he'd taken shelter yesterday. A section of grass close to the river was blackened where the lightning had touched down.

Razor's head came up.

"It's okay." Caleb patted his mount's neck. "I know this place makes you nervous, but there's nothing here now."

He'd lain awake last night going over in his head Kaye's limited confession. Flashbacks were normal, and that was what worried him if he got back in the arena with bucking horses—he might freeze up, leaving the cowboy hanging. He worked in tandem with another pick-up rider, but moments made the difference in saving a cowboy and him being hurt.

When the sound of another rider pierced his brain, he turned in his saddle and saw Joel riding toward him. "Any cattle down here?"

Shaking off the memories, Caleb answered, "I haven't looked yet."

Joel's brow knitted into a frown. He scanned the area and saw the blackened spot down by the stream. "Is this where you and my sister took shelter?"

"No, it was in the stand of trees there." He pointed.

Leaning on the saddle horn, Joel asked, "Did something else happen here? Sis kinda looked panicked when I asked where you two were."

Caleb knew Kaye didn't want her brother to know about her flashback, but Joel's friendship meant a great deal to him. And Caleb knew if his brother had a need, he would want to know. "Let's say that you should pray for your sister."

"What's that supposed to mean?"

"I know you know how to pray, and you might pray for me, too."

Joel sat up, ready to press more questions.

"Let's see if there are any strays down here." Before Joel could comment, Caleb headed down to the river. If his friend questioned him too much, he just might guess what happened, and Caleb wouldn't do that to Kaye.

Anything that was electronic in the house was fried. They documented every appliance and lamp. Thankfully, Joel's laptop hadn't been charging or they would've lost all the rodeo information, too. As Bryan took pictures of the damage, he updated Kaye on nearly all the sixty kids who'd been in their graduating class. Bryan took pictures of the porch and had Kaye sign the report.

"Can we start the cleanup of the porch?" Kaye asked, Gramps standing behind her. The charred smell brought too many memories.

"Yes, since I've got everything documented here. And those cell phone pictures, you can email them to me. By Friday, I should have the check for you, so do you need anything before then?"

"You going to be delivering dinner for us?" Gramps asked.

Bryan looked like he'd run into a wall but quickly recovered. "You were always a teaser, weren't you, Mr. Kaye?"

Gramps scowled. "I wasn't teasing. We've got no way to keep anything cold, and peanut-butter sandwiches aren't on my list—"

Kaye touched Gramps's arm. "You should probably get

another cup of coffee, Gramps. I'll hash things out with Bryan."

With his lips pursed in a straight line, Gramps eyed the insurance adjuster and walked away.

"Did your grandfather get those bruises when the lightning strike happened?"

"No." She explained about the accident. "I'm sorry, Bryan, Gramps is a little off his stride."

"I understand. If a tractor fell on me and all the appliances in my house got fried, I'd be a little out of sorts, too." He walked to his car, opened his trunk and pulled two hundred dollars out of a cash box. "This is for immediate expenses. If you need anything else, call."

After Bryan finished, Kaye walked around the house and made a list of what needed to be replaced. Joel called, telling Kaye fences were down and cattle scattered. They needed to round them up. Kaye took pity on him and told him they couldn't get the insurance money until Friday, so they'd shop on Saturday after the meeting.

That night, Cheryl, Bryan's wife, drove up to the house and delivered a pot of stew and biscuits.

Kaye hugged Cheryl, thanking her.

"That's what neighbors are for. I'm glad to see you home."

When they sat down for dinner, Kaye nailed Gramps with a look. "Did you thank Cheryl?"

Both Joel's and Caleb's eyes widened and they exchanged panicked looks.

Gramps put down his spoon. "I did. I thanked her and told her to thank her husband for the help. Sometimes I'm a cranky old man. Cheryl laughed and kissed my cheek."

"Good for you, Gramps."

After dinner, Joel, Caleb and Kaye worked on cleaning the porch. Gramps wanted to help, but Kaye convinced him if he sat in the kitchen chair on the porch and directed the work, it would be better.

Caleb could only marvel at Kaye's ability to change Gramps's mind.

"She's good," Caleb whispered as Joel handed Caleb a push broom.

"That's why I wanted her to do the rodeo." Joel looked over his shoulder as Kaye settled Gramps into the chair.

"Okay, can you see from there, Gramps?" Kaye asked.

"I can, but y'all need to get moving. Sun's going down and we don't have light."

Caleb wanted to laugh. Kaye didn't take offense. The three of them worked together. Joel got on a ladder and looked at the roof. He took a broom with him and from his perch pushed debris through the remains of the roof. Caleb picked up the large shingles and pieces of wood. Kaye swept the floor.

Caleb caught Kaye pausing, and he watched her struggle with her emotions. When she looked up, there weren't tears in her eyes as he expected, but determination. She finished sweeping, and if he hadn't seen her "moment" he never would've known how she felt. Joel and Gramps didn't see it, but he did and somehow, some way, she touched his heart in a way he didn't understand, leaving him confused and wary.

The whirlwind of more insurance adjusters, repairmen and visits to the local hardware store became a blessing for Kaye over the next two days because the instant she stopped, she'd see something her mother or grandmother loved and the memories assaulted her, bruising her heart. They were heartaches and feelings she wasn't ready to deal with.

Kaye made trips to the store for ice, where she discovered their neighbor to the north, John Burkett, had also had a lightning strike. It had hit a tree, and the tree had taken out the corner of their house, but other than Burkett Ranch, every other rancher had escaped damage from the storm.

At nine o'clock Saturday morning, Joel, Gramps, Caleb and Kaye walked into the Country Kitchen Café in downtown Peaster. Nan White, Mike Johnson and Laurie Benson sat at a table in the back. The little café was one of the few buildings that hadn't changed. The town had doubled in size. There was a big chain hardware store and a new building called Marten Orchards, which boasted the best peaches in the county. Kaye felt like an outsider in her own hometown.

Mike waved to the group. As Joel passed the waitress, he said, "Annie, we need four cups of coffee and some of those famous sticky rolls you got here."

Those rolls Kaye remembered with great anticipation.

The waitress nodded and walked away. Someone else she didn't know.

They scooted into the long red vinyl bench at the back of the restaurant. Sandwiched between Caleb and her brother, Kaye felt every inch of Caleb beside her. She frowned at him.

"Is something wrong?"

"No." Feeling stupid, she admitted to herself she hadn't been this aware of another male since the first night she went for coffee with her now-ex after their class.

Joel made the introductions. "And this is Laurie Benson. She and her husband bought the Blanchard Ranch the year after you graduated."

Once coffee and rolls were delivered, Joel started the meeting. "My sister has volunteered to take over for me as the chairman of this rodeo. When she was in the army, she did this kind of thing all the time and was good."

He laid it on thick, but her brother's praise warmed Kaye's heart.

Every eye focused on her. She especially felt Caleb's gaze, but the vibes of the other three board members were doubtful.

Oddly enough, Nan went to bat for her. "When Kaye called me the other morning, we talked. She had some good ideas on how to organize this thing. I was getting nervous about what my job was and how we were going to get things done."

Joel drew back as if insulted.

Nan's spine stiffened. "Well, you haven't done anything yet. Charm can only get you so far."

Kaye choked on her coffee. Caleb patted her on the back.

"Sorry," she mumbled.

"Anyway," Nan continued. "I liked her ideas. You need to hear them."

Kaye felt in her element, comfortable organizing an event and welcomed the chance to put her skills to work. "I've gone over everything and wanted to get your input. I thought we would organize things this morning, assign tasks and set out deadlines."

The other members agreed and for the next three hours they hashed out details, chores, set dates and organized a charity rodeo, much to the satisfaction of all the board members.

Caleb stood back and watched in awe as Kaye finished negotiating the final deal on the new sixty-inch TV. When the middle-aged salesman had first approached her, his attitude had been "let's appease the little lady." When he'd addressed his questions about buying the matched washer/dryer set to Joel, Kaye had stepped in and corrected him. She didn't use harsh words but firmly let the salesman know she made the final decision. The salesman had quickly changed his tune. Caleb nearly laughed out loud at the man's expression.

"Yes, ma'am. We'll have it out to your ranch Monday," the man said.

"Thank you, Morgan." She'd learned the man's name and used it liberally.

Her skill in handling the salesman startled Caleb. She was a force unto herself, which clashed with the woman he'd held in his arms during that storm. This was no indecisive woman. No, this was a woman who meant business. As if he needed another demonstration of Kaye's skill after the morning meeting at the café.

"She continues to amaze me," Joel whispered. "When we were growing up, I saw some flashes of that strong will, but I could still get my way or fool her."

"I wouldn't try it now."

Joel rubbed his chin. "No, I'm still going to challenge her. That's what big brothers do."

"I'll give you that. My brother may have graduated with his masters, but I'm still the oldest."

"You understand. Still, I'm amazed by her and how she's fought back against the odds."

Caleb understood his friend's feelings.

"I worried, praying that she didn't get buried in what happened to her. Everything seemed good until you asked me to pray. You got me worried again." He rubbed his hand behind his neck. "Growing up, I tried to protect her—" He fell silent.

Caleb knew how hard it was to see a sibling hurt. He remembered seeing his brother sporting bruises their mom's latest boyfriend had given Sawyer while Caleb had been gone, working his shift at the feed store after school.

Joel took a deep breath. "I'm glad to have her home." His chest puffed out. "She's a fighter."

Yes, the woman was a fighter, which made what had happened in the thunderstorm all that more heart wrenching.

She glanced at Caleb and smiled. He gave her a thumbs-up.

"Brenda?"

Kaye stiffened.

"Brenda Lynn Kaye." A woman darted around several TV stands. "Is that you?" she squealed, enveloping Kaye in a big hug.

When the stranger pulled back, Kaye said, "Billye Ludwig?"

"It's Zimmerman now. Of course, after the divorce I should go back to Ludwig." The woman shook off her frown. "What are you doing here?" She looked Kaye up and down. "You still in the army?"

"No. I'm a civilian now."

"When did that happen? I thought you were a lifer."

Before Kaye could respond, a little girl about five and a boy, seven or eight, walked up to the women. Billye wrapped her arms around both kids.

"Brenda, I want you to meet my children, Amanda and Stewart. Kids, this is my best friend from high school, Brenda Kaye."

A fleeting expression of sorrow entered Kaye's eyes. She quickly masked it and greeted each child, making sure she listened to them.

"Mom, I'm hungry," Amanda complained, pulling on her mother's jeans.

"Okay, kids. Let me have your number, Brenda, and let's set up a lunch. I'd love to chat and hear about your life in the army. It had to be so much more exciting than being stuck here."

After exchanging numbers, Billye waved and they were gone.

Kaye took a deep breath and turned toward them. Whatever she'd been feeling, she pushed it down. "If you're ready, we still have some shopping to do. I know Joel needs his hair dryer, and I don't think we can buy it here."

Joel frowned at her. "What are you talking about?"

Kaye wrapped her arm around her brother's and pulled him to the front of the store. "The hair dryer I found in your bathroom that was fried."

Joel swallowed any further protest.

Caleb bit back his grin. Joel Kaye used a hair dryer. Good ammunition and Kaye used it well.

The lady was amazing. The kind of woman he always knew he wanted to marry. He stopped the thought cold.

What in the Sam Hill was he thinking?

Chapter Five

The final amen of the service rang through the church.

"One more thing," Pastor Tom said, holding up his hand, stopping the congregation from spilling out of the pews. "I want to welcome home Captain Brenda Kaye. She grew up in this church, and although I came after she left, I've heard only good things about her."

The congregation applauded.

Her gaze clashed with Joel's. He shrugged, but an impish smile curved his mouth.

"And according to her brother, Joel, she's taken over the charity rodeo that we're going to hold in May. Brenda, would you like to come up here and tell the congregation a little more about it?"

Kaye felt an uncontrollable urge to kick her brother. "You could've warned me," she whispered.

Joel's grin just widened. She looked at Caleb. He shrugged. "You're up to it."

Gramps waved her up to the dais.

Kaye made her way to the front of the church and faced the congregation, recognizing half the people sitting in the pews. "Since I was drafted to head this event, I've discovered we're going to need lots of help. When I was in the army, part of my job was to organize events, so after it was explained to me why we were holding the rodeo, I was happy to do it. I'm sure plenty of you want to help, too, and I welcome and encourage it.

"If the pastor will allow us the use of the fellowship hall, we could meet this coming week—" She glanced at the pastor.

"Tuesday would be good."

"Tuesday, and I'll be ready to do sign ups and the other members of the board can be there, too."

Pastor Tom nodded. "Well, while we're at it, why don't we make it a potluck dinner?"

There were several nods in the audience.

"All right, we'll meet at six-thirty. Bring your best dish and be ready to sign up to work."

The organist played the final hymn. Pastor Tom shook her hand. "I'm glad the church will get involved, because my heart's been burdened for our ranchers and I've been thinking of different ways to help. And all have been praying for some way to help our ranchers. I think this may be it."

When Kaye walked out into the churchyard, she discovered no one had left. Excitement filled the air with people clustered in groups, talking about the rodeo. Outside a dozen people came up to her, offering their help, then sympathized with Gramps over the bruising on his face and his arm in the sling. Several high school friends reintroduced themselves to Kaye and offered suggestions on the rodeo. Most she recognized, but a few she didn't know until they said their name.

They decided to eat in town since they still had no stove. The First Community Church stood at the north end of Main Street while at the other end was the new municipal building, the Sweet Treats Shop and the county fairgrounds. The Country Kitchen Café occupied the building midway between the church and municipal building. They walked to the café.

It didn't take long for word to spread about the Tuesday meeting for sign ups, and by the end of their lunch, fifteen individuals from different congregations had stopped by their table, offering their help.

Tuesday night, the fellowship hall at First Community Church was packed. People who were not part of their congregation showed up. Kaye's heart overflowed as she stared at the gathering. These were ranchers from around the area, businessmen from town and city workers. The other members of the board were as amazed as Kaye. Even the manager of the county fairgrounds was there. One rancher, who was from outside of Waco, came up and introduced himself. He'd heard about the rodeo from his cousin who lived here. Kaye had to keep her jaw from going slack and shook the man's hand.

"Wow," Caleb whispered. "This is quite a turnout."

"These are our neighbors." Joel's eyes scanned each face and pride radiated off him.

"And friends. Ranchers," Gramps added. "They all have faced hardships and are willing to help others in the same situation because they've faced it themselves."

The evening passed quickly, with everyone in the fellowship hall finding something they could do or offering to provide some service. The concession people offered to give any profit they might make to the cause of buying seed. Several of the adults who worked in Fort Worth offered to tell their coworkers about the rodeo, and Kaye set up a meeting with the fairground manager for the next day. The work the planning committee had done the previous Saturday came in handy, since they were able to divide up the volunteers among the different committees of registration, booths, housing, fairgrounds and volunteers for the two days of the event.

As they drove back from the meeting, Kaye closed her eyes.

"See, Sis, you're going to have help."

Kaye opened one eye and stared at her brother in the driver's seat. "Are you trying to ease over throwing me to the lions?"

He looked into the rearview mirror. "No, but you see, everyone in this county is willing to help."

"So I can put you in charge of getting the stock for the different rodeo events?"

Gramps tapped Joel on the shoulder. "She's got you there."

Caleb, who was in the backseat with Kaye, shook his head.

"Really, Caleb would be better at doing that than me," Joel argued, "since he's been working the rodeo for the past few years. He's more knowledgeable, got more current connections."

Caleb glared at his friend. "Are you pushing things off on me?"

"No. But you know the suppliers and have worked around them much more than I have recently."

"He's got a point," Gramps offered from the front passenger seat.

Caleb laughed and shook his head.

"Are you going to let him get away with that?" Kaye leaned close and whispered. That was a mistake because Caleb's own unique scent filled her lungs. He turned his head toward her and his lips were a breath's distance from hers.

"I shouldn't, but when he's right, he's right. I think I can arrange things with a supplier I know."

Joel grinned into the rearview mirror, his expression letting Kaye know he knew best.

"You sure you want to let him railroad you, too?" she said, gazing back into Caleb's intense green gaze.

She remembered how it felt to be held in his arms and her heart filled with longing. She was a woman whom others depended upon, but there were times when she needed to be gathered into sheltering arms and given comfort. Her ex had never understood that. He'd expected her to always be strong and be there for him.

She saw Caleb's Adam's apple bob as he swallowed. The electricity in the backseat felt like the atmosphere before the lightning had struck.

"It's the least I can do." He grabbed her hand and squeezed it.

"Hey, break it up back there," Joel called out.

Caleb smirked. "Mind your own business."

"I am," Joel replied.

Kaye met her brother's gaze in the rearview mirror and glared.

He laughed it off.

"I hope you're not disappointed you lost the coin toss and had to come with me," Kaye told Caleb as they drove to the county fairgrounds the next morning.

"It's probably best that I came since I'm the one arranging for the supplier to bring the stock, and the fairgrounds will have requirements they want the supplier to meet."

Caleb spent a lot of mornings sharing coffee with different rodeo managers, listening to the problems they were dealing with. Joel wouldn't know the current ins and outs of the rodeo world like he did. He felt guilty for not working as her pick-up rider, but the accident had shaken him to the core and he just wasn't ready. This, however, he could do.

"I'll say that turnout yesterday was impressive."

"True," Kaye said. "But when I thought about it, it's not surprising. Ranch folks are generous and willing to help."

"You're right." He knew from experience how generous ranchers were. He and his brother, Sawyer, had been at the receiving end of such generosity with the congregation in Plainview, up in the panhandle of the state.

"Turn here," Kaye said. "It'll be interesting to see the county fairgrounds and how they've changed."

He turned down the gravel road. "You've been here before?"

"If you grew up in this city, you came to the fairgrounds. Of course, in October, when they had the State Fair in Dallas, we drove to Fair Park and showed stock and my brother's 4-H project."

"And did you have one?"

"Of course. If you went to school in our school district, you had a 4-H project. I had a lamb."

"You win anything?"

"No, but going to the fair was the highlight of the year. Corny dogs and fresh-squeezed lemonade. That was to die for."

He didn't believe his ears. "You mean after all the places you've been with the army, corny dogs at the State Fair is your favorite food?"

She grinned, making him catch his breath. "I do."

"Hard to believe."

He turned into the parking lot of the fairgrounds and drove to the entrance. A stadium surrounded by bleachers occupied the middle of the area. Around it, closed booths stood silent, waiting for visitors to come back. Cattle pens were on the far end of the fairgrounds.

"Obviously you haven't had a corny dog at the fair. We can fix that this October."

Her comment caught him off guard. He doubted he would be here in October, but he liked the sound of that promise.

"'Course, you'll get to witness our rodeo/county fair this year. Most of the ranchers' wives come and sell something. I remember Mrs. Johnson sold her canned tomatoes and pickles. Mrs. Lions sold the blankets she knitted. And Mrs. Plasek sold her homemade Polish sausage. It was delicious. And Mrs. Rivera sold apricot empanadas."

They were good childhood memories, unlike his. But the folks of Plainview had filled Sawyer's and his bellies with good home cooking. The pastor's wife made a mean chocolate cake, and she'd taken to bringing cookies, cakes and homemade bread to the apartment behind the church for the two teenage boys.

"I'll be looking forward to experiencing those foods again." She exited the truck and started toward the fair entrance. "Of course, I wonder if all those ranchers are still here. I kinda lost track."

He followed her into the fairgrounds and they headed toward the bleachers. "I know there used to be an office close to the stands."

Before they reached the office, Ken Moody called to them. They turned around and saw him coming in from the parking lot. "I'm sorry I forgot to tell you, Brenda, that my office is in town now."

She stiffened when Ken said her given name. "I'm used to going by Kaye. I'll respond quicker if you use that."

He nodded. "I understand. It's been a while since you've been here." He shook their hands. "Let me show you around to see how we've changed and improved things, then we can go back to my office and work out a plan."

"Sounds good."

Forty-five minutes later, they walked into the city hall where Ken's office was now located. People stopped them in the municipal building to add to the congratulations and give suggestions on what to include or what not to forget. Excitement and hopeful attitudes seemed to be floating in the air. The mayor joined the meeting with Ken and Kaye and Caleb.

"I'll call a friend of mine who is an animal supplier," Caleb told the group. "I've worked with him for the past four years and asked if he could help. I think he might do this event for cost. And maybe we can get the feed donated."

"Since I own the sign shop in town," Mayor Asa Kitridge added, "I'll donate signs for the event, before and after."

"Can you do business cards for the rodeo?" Kaye asked. "We could hand them out and have the information people needed to either participate or just come and watch the rodeo." Kaye looked from one man to the other.

"I like how you think." Asa grabbed a piece of paper off Ken's desk and scribbled the information. "That looks good." He glanced around the group. All nodded.

"Good. I can have those business cards in a couple days. As a matter of fact, I'll work up the template and send it to y'all in an email."

"Use Joel's email," Kaye supplied.

"And I'll notify others in the fair association what we're doing," Caleb added. "They can talk to members of the Professional Rodeo Cowboy Association and see if we can get any PRCA participants."

They shook hands, all buoyed by the meeting. As they were leaving, Mayor Kitridge slapped Caleb on the back. "I'm glad you'll be working the rodeo. That accident in

Albuquerque could've happened to anyone. How is that cowboy, by the way?"

If Asa had chosen to stab him with a knife in his gut, the pain couldn't have been worse. Caleb paled. "The last I heard, Taggert was doing okay, but I'm not going to work as the pick-up rider."

"Oh," Asa said. "Sorry. I didn't mean to bring up a sore subject."

Gathering his wits, Caleb nodded. "There are several guys I can contact that would do it. I'll get someone."

The mayor quickly made his goodbyes and walked out of the building.

Kaye didn't question Caleb on the ride back to the ranch. He appreciated her discretion. He still wasn't ready to talk about the accident, but if other cowboys were coming to compete, she'd hear.

"You're quiet," he started out.

"We got a lot accomplished this morning. And I'll let Joel know how much you are doing. He needs to start pulling his weight. He is not getting off scot-free. I'm going to keep him honest."

"He needs a taskmaster." He waited for the follow-up on the mayor's question, but she pulled out her list and went over it. She wasn't going to push about the accident. He could breathe easier. The lady had good instincts.

As they pulled up in front of the farmhouse, there was a truck there from the big home-improvement store, unloading their earlier purchases. Gramps stood out on the porch, a frown on his bruised face.

"About time you showed up, missy. Come in and show the guys how you want things arranged. They're having trouble and asking me what to do, like I know what to do in the kitchen. And they kept saying something about an electrician."

She turned to Caleb. "If any of the men under my command heard Gramps talk to me like that, I'd never live it down." She slipped out of the truck.

Caleb knew that those men would realize that Kaye had a grandfather who loved her and wouldn't doubt her strength in leading. He'd seen her frightened and disoriented, but that didn't stop this woman.

Her strength amazed him and drew him in. She simply accepted he wouldn't work as the pick-up rider. She didn't cry or question or try to manipulate him. She honored his decision. Had he ever run into a woman like that? His mother had whining down to an art and would keep at a man until he gave in. After his dad died, that was how she dealt with the series of boyfriends that paraded through their lives.

His heart protested being locked away by memories of a mother who used others and the rodeo bunnies that used the cowboys on the circuit for their own purposes. He'd retreated to the Kaye ranch to have time to think and consider his future, and suddenly this beautiful woman had shown up. He had to admit to himself he liked the feel of Kaye in his arms. Was heaven showing him a different path?

Was his heart telling him it was time?

He didn't know.

Chapter Six

The last of the deliverymen wheeled out her mother's old washer to his truck.

"This was a good machine. Thirty years. My mom still has hers." The deliveryman shook his head. "But a lightning strike will zap anything."

His words robbed Kaye of breath. She stared at the top-loading Maytag. She remembered her mom standing over it, feeding her dad's jeans into that machine.

"You the lady organizing the charity rodeo?" he asked.

His question snapped her out of the past. "I am."

"What if my brother wanted to sign up for bareback ridin'?"

Mike Johnson, one of the directors, was in charge of the website and registration. "The website should be up now and you can register online." She gave him the web address of the charity rodeo. "Or stop by the mayor's office or print shop. You'll find the information there."

"I'll let my brother know." He climbed in his truck and drove away.

Kaye shook off the sad memories evoked by the washing machine's removal and started toward the house. What had happened to Gramps? Had he ridden out to help Joel?

Surely not. Gramps still was in no condition to be on a horse. Anxiety high, she searched the house but didn't find him. Charging out to the barn, Kaye readied herself to either hop on a horse or four-wheeler to fetch her delinquent grandfather. She'd just built up a good head of steam when she found Gramps asleep on a hay bale, leaning against the barn wall.

Tenderness welled in her heart. Gramps would never admit he needed a nap, that his age was catching up to him, but out here, he could sleep without her knowing about it and save his pride.

She walked back to the house, entering the kitchen. The new appliances stuck out like neon lights nestled among the aged cabinets and pitted '60s pea-green Formica countertops. A sparkling new toaster sat on the countertop along with a new coffeemaker.

They're beautiful. Her mother's voice rang in her head. She could see her mom preening over the new, beautiful appliances. Moisture gathered in her eyes and Kaye's lips quivered. "Oh, Mom, you'd be so proud," she whispered.

And her father would've been just as proud for his wife. Although there were years when there was no money for extras, her dad's generous heart had always managed to pamper his wife.

The ache grew and Kaye fought for breath. She stumbled out the back door, but her legs only carried her to the charred picnic table. Memories flashed through her head like a kaleidoscope of birthdays, Christmases, spring roundup. She fought the grief and longing for her parents and grandmother that she'd been able to ignore or suppress since she'd left home. Closing her eyes, the memories continued to pummel her....

"Kaye? Are you all right?"

She heard Caleb's words through the layers of sorrow.

She felt him sit beside her and turned to him to assure him she was fine. Tears blinded her vision and her chest heaved. The next thing she knew, she heard someone crying and didn't realize it was her until Caleb pulled her into his arms and cradled her head tenderly on his shoulder.

The pain and grief rolled out of her, much like floodgates opening, and she had no control over them.

How long she cried, she couldn't say, but it seemed like hours. When sanity returned, she felt the support and comfort of Caleb's arms. This was the second time the man had held her and surrounded her with his strength.

She pulled away, wiping her face. A choked laugh escaped her as she shook her head. "You'd never believe I was an efficient military officer who never once cried the entire time I was in the army. I didn't even cry when my ex emailed me, telling me he was filing for divorce."

Well, she'd certainly put it all out there, hadn't she?

"I believe you."

His response brought her gaze up to his. Was he pulling her leg? She studied him. "Really?"

"My mom was someone who couldn't cope with anything after my father died. You, Kaye, are nothing like her. From what I've seen, you're doing fine."

She couldn't quite believe her ears. "It was seeing all those new appliances in the kitchen. I knew my mom would've been so excited and suddenly it just blindsided me." She looked down at her hands. "Coming home, there are so many memories. When you're dead tired from a day of basic training, your brain doesn't work. You just fall unconscious into your bunk.

"I took the coward's way out when I left here."

Caleb's finger lifted her chin. "I don't see a coward. I see an amazingly strong woman who has dealt with a lot of tragedy."

She searched his face, trying to see if he really meant what he said. His eyes held admiration and something else.

Embarrassed, she looked away.

Gramps walked out of the barn. "The deliverymen finished in the house?"

"They're gone, Gramps."

"Well, let me go in and test out the new TV." He started up the porch stairs. "You coming?"

She looked at Gramps over Caleb's shoulder. "I am. And you can show Caleb your new toy."

Gramps walked inside. As Kaye stood, Caleb said, "Give yourself a break, Kaye. You've held it together much better than anyone else I've known."

But not good enough. "Thanks."

As they walked into the house, Kaye knew the ground under her had shifted, but she wasn't ready to acknowledge how it had moved.

"It's nice to have a full meal for a change." Joel sighed as he and Caleb sat on the stairs to the back porch after dinner. Kaye had used the new stove to cook spaghetti, but she'd insisted the men make the salad. They'd also cleaned the porch and would fix the roof this weekend. "And it's nice not to have to cook."

Caleb shook his head. "I guess you need to get married, friend."

Joel drew back. "Me? What about you?"

Caleb didn't have a quick comeback.

Joel, his elbows resting on his knees, turned his head, meeting his friend's gaze. "What, no comeback?"

A deep sigh escaped Caleb's chest. "You know when you get an itch. You're going along and everything is fine, then *wham,* it all blows up."

Joel nodded. "I hear ya."

"I've had that itch since Sawyer finished school." He ran his hand through his hair. "Even before Albuquerque, I've been restless, wondering if I want to keep living out of my horse trailer and not having roots.

"You had a home to come back to when you stopped. I've been toying for some time with finding a ranch and breeding stock for the rodeo. I know Jack Murphy is always looking for good stock for the rodeos he supplies. After the rodeo in Lubbock this past spring, Jack complained he needed more ranchers he could buy stock from."

"You serious?"

"My need for a steady income changed with Sawyer out working, using that new degree. And I'm tired of living like a gypsy. I've been doing this for the past sixteen years. For the past year, I've been socking away most of my paychecks and saved up enough money to buy a place."

"Is that the only reason you've stayed so long this time?"

Caleb looked away. "My body's starting to complain about the traveling, eating in different places, and I got aches I never had before. Staying put is looking mighty good." At least that was what he'd been telling himself since the accident.

"You know that what happened in Albuquerque wasn't your fault, don't you?" Joel pressed.

Caleb recovered from the gut punch. Surely he could've done something different to avoid what happened.

Joel nailed him with a look that said he knew the guilt Caleb lived with. "You've got to deal with it."

Caleb stilled, not believing his friend was pressing this.

"I don't mean to push."

Caleb stood. "Good."

Joel raised his hands, surrendering the topic.

Feeling foolish, Caleb sat. "You know of any ranches around here for sale?"

"Yeah, there's a lot. There's a drought, too. You sure you want those headaches?"

"Good question." He thought for a moment. "Why don't you go back out on the circuit and I'll buy this place."

Joel laughed. "You'd have to take Gramps with it. Maybe even my sis."

The teasing comment hit Caleb between the eyes. A family. Gramps and Kaye. It sounded so good. Sawyer and he had never had grandparents they knew. Neither his father nor mother's families had been in the picture when he was growing up. He'd known about his dad's parents and vaguely remembered visiting them in Tucumcari, but precious little had been said about his mother's parents. "Sounds good."

Joel's head jerked around. "I was teasing."

"I know." But the idea grabbed his soul. A home. A family. A wife. Kaye.

They heard the back door slam and they looked up to see Kaye.

"Gramps could use some help getting ready for bed."

Joel stood. "I'll see y'all tomorrow morning." He walked back into the kitchen.

Kaye settled on the step Joel had vacated. "I would've helped Gramps, but he wasn't even going near that suggestion. He acted insulted."

Caleb laughed. "You're dealing with a different generation."

She smiled and shook her head.

Sitting next to her brought back memories of her in his arms this afternoon, crying. Of course, as she'd cooked dinner, no one would've known about her emotional breakdown. That intrigued him. "We got a lot accomplished today—the morning sessions in town and the afternoon deliveries."

"We did. I even had one of the deliverymen asking how his brother could register to compete in the rodeo."

"That's great news. Word of mouth has gotten around this town."

"And this is one time I'm glad that word of mouth spread so quickly through the county."

There was pain in that last comment, but he decided to leave it alone. "So do you want to go with all the events that the mayor suggested?" They talked about tie-down roping, team roping, bareback riding, steer wrestling, bull riding, barrel racing and saddle bronc riding.

"If we could get enough entrants. I'll talk to Mike about it. But I'll add calf scramble for the kids, and I loved the idea of a celebrity pin-a-calf event."

"Have the sheriff's department versus the volunteer fire department?"

She smiled, and he felt it in his gut.

"I like that. And maybe have teen girls versus teen boys." She rubbed her hands together.

Caleb could see that. "That's a win for the guys."

"In your dreams, cowboy," she shot back.

He threw his head back and laughed. She joined him. He welcomed that fighting spirit of hers. He thought of her all afternoon, understanding how sometimes events could slap you up the side of the head. He'd wondered if she would be moody when they ate dinner, much like his mother had been. But if he hadn't held her while she cried, he wouldn't have known about her tears. The lady fought back.

"So you think the girls will outdo the boys?" He arched his brow.

"I wouldn't count them out. In the army, there are some jobs that women do better than their male counterparts."

"But with that brute-strength thing, guys have the advantage." Mirth danced in his eyes.

"You'd be surprised, cowboy. I knew a couple women who could take down any man." She tapped her chin. "I remember we had a drill instructor. She took down a man who jumped on her when she was leaving a restaurant. She put the man in the hospital."

They sat quietly as evening turned to night before them. "There's nothing better than watching the moon rise from my own back porch." She leaned toward him. "But I'll say that when I was in Albuquerque, watching the moon rise there at that elevation, the sky looks different."

"Albuquerque?" he choked out. What had she being doing in that city?

She turned and a small frown gathered between her brows. "That's where the equine therapy ranch I spent time at was."

"Oh."

"It's amazing out there seeing the moon on a clear, cold night at that mile-high elevation, but there's something about seeing the moon in your own backyard that makes it special. Didn't you ever sit outside and watch the moon rise?"

"Yeah." He remembered once when his mother's boyfriend at the time had slapped Sawyer. Caleb had stood up to the man and got a good beating. Both he and Sawyer had left the house and walked out into the pasture behind their house. They'd slept outside that spring night. Through his puffy eyes, he'd seen a harvest moon rise and it had been as if God had sent him comfort, telling Caleb that he wasn't forgotten. Caleb had known then he would take Sawyer and leave when he had saved enough money.

Her hand covered his. "Thanks for this afternoon."

"No problem. After we finish this rodeo, you have any idea what you might do?"

"Well, I've been toying with the idea of getting my

counseling certificate. While I was in the army, I got my college degree in business administration. I also had a major in psychology and social work."

"That's impressive."

"Naw, but I'd like to see what it would take to get my certificate to counsel other vets. I know there's a need." She hung her head. "Maybe I can talk to myself and counsel myself. Or pray. Of course, prayer does wonders, but first you have to do it."

He took her hand in his, interlacing their fingers.

"I guess I should get some benefit from my degree aside from an ex-husband."

She gained his attention.

"So you said." Oddly, he felt the need to push. Or maybe Kaye needed to talk.

A frown gathered between her brows. "You sure you don't have your degree in counseling? I mean, every time I'm around you, I spill my guts. *This* has got to stop."

"Guess I'm just a sympathetic guy."

"Really?"

"I'm a good listener."

She pursed her lips. She remained silent for so long, he thought she wouldn't say anything. "I was stationed in Alabama. Since I went to OTS—Officer Training School for all you nonmilitary types—they give their officers an opportunity to get a bachelor's degree. I couldn't resist. When I was in psych class, I got to know one of the guys in the class. We hit it off. He played in a band. Richard made me laugh. And he was a good guitar player. I went and listened to him play a gig and was impressed.

"It was a whirlwind romance and we married. It was a sort of spur-of-the-moment thing, and Joel and Gramps didn't have time to drive to Alabama before the wedding." Her words stopped and she tugged her hand.

Caleb loosened his grip and she pulled her hand away. "His band started being successful, playing different clubs around the South. I guess Richard thought I'd resign my commission. He dropped out of school and started traveling with the band full-time." She turned to him. "I understood his need to perform, to travel, but you have to have money. If it hadn't been for my paycheck and the PX, well, we would've starved. Then when I got my orders to go to Ft. Drum in New York, he wouldn't go with me. I called him after work one day and a young woman answered. She handed him the phone and he told me he wanted a divorce.

"Thankfully, the judge didn't order me to pay him alimony. Once I was in Iraq, I thanked my army lawyer that I had that divorce decree, but my ex didn't let that stop him and used our joint credit card, although I'd canceled it. They tried coming after me. They didn't get far."

"I'm sorry you had to go through that." She told the story without any of the "poor me" attitude his mother would've used.

"I don't know what happened to my judgment." She pursed her lips. "But I'm not going to make that mistake again."

It sounded like her ex had done a number on her. Of course, with what she told him, she was better off without the man. But it didn't sound like she was in any mood to try again.

Although he wasn't in any better position for a romance so he need not worry. But he needed to tell his heart to stop noticing what a strong, beautiful woman Kaye was. The type he'd always wanted.

Kaye couldn't believe her mouth. It seemed every time she was within earshot of Caleb, things tumbled out that she hadn't told another soul. It was time to turn the tables on him.

"So what are you going to do after our charity event? You plan on going back to the rodeo?"

His expression sobered. Their easy exchange stopped and he put up a barrier. "I don't know. I'm starting to get a little too old to be constantly traveling and living out of my trailer. I've discovered aches and pains that weren't there before. Getting up in the morning is a challenge."

"What did your dad do? Maybe you could follow in his footsteps."

He looked down at his hands. "He worked on a ranch near San Antonio."

She waited for more of an explanation.

"Pops died of a heart attack when I was twelve. I would've loved to talk to him about ranching. He didn't own the place, but he competed in rodeos to get extra money. He wanted to buy his own spread."

She wondered about his mother, but from his body language, he wouldn't welcome the question. "Well, it seems you and I are facing some massive changes in our lives."

"More like circumstances made that change for us."

"Bad circumstances."

He shrugged. "There are lots of bad things that happen to people. I wondered why my dad died so suddenly. After wrestling with that question for several years, my pastor said we are still humans even after we believe. It's what we do with the tragedy and grief that we have control over, and do we give to Him who can heal our hearts the grief and tragedy."

She heard what he said, but her heart wasn't buying. "There had to be a reason. It's not just chance. It can't be." Angry, she stood abruptly and walked into the house.

* * *

Kaye couldn't sleep. Every time she closed her eyes, she'd remember how she broke down in front of Caleb that afternoon. She'd bawled, losing it completely. And combined with that earlier incident in the storm, what was wrong with her? She wasn't eighteen anymore, so why was she acting that way? Suddenly, she didn't recognize herself.

She remembered Caleb's sheltering arms, giving strength and comfort. The man always seemed to be there, unlike her ex. When she'd wanted to cuddle with her ex after a long, rough day, he'd looked at her as if he couldn't be bothered.

Finally, Kaye gave up, threw off her covers, pulled on her robe and padded into the kitchen. The chocolate-chip cookies she'd seen in the pantry were calling her.

At the kitchen door she stopped. Gramps sat at the table, several cookies before him. He looked up. "It seems great minds think alike."

She wanted to laugh. "I don't know about that, but hungry stomachs tend to react the same way." She snagged a few cookies, poured herself some milk and joined Gramps at the table. "We've done this before."

"We have. You were a squirt and couldn't sleep, excited about Christmas. I often wondered if you planned to sneak in the living room and see what Santa brought you."

Gramps and Grandma had spent Christmas Eve with them, then her dad and Gramps did the chores before they opened Christmas presents.

"I could never fool you." Those words took on another meaning. She knew in her gut Gramps had seen Caleb holding her this afternoon.

Suddenly, her cookie held enormous interest. He waited, not pushing.

"What's going on between you and that fine man?" Gramps asked.

Her head jerked up. "What?"

"I saw Caleb holding you."

"Nothing's going on between us." She cleared her throat. "I was blue about Mom's and Grandma's appliances being hauled away. He sat next to me and asked what was wrong. When I turned to him, well, the tears kinda came on their own. I was embarrassed by it. There was no way I'd have cried in the service."

He nodded and she realized he'd gotten her to admit she was having trouble with the memories.

He didn't have on his sling and laid his hand on hers. "Joel and I know you've never made peace with losing your parents and grandmother."

She opened her mouth to object, but Gramps's stern look stopped her.

"I know your parents and grandmother wouldn't want you to suffer that way. You need to make peace with those memories. And I guarantee you that if you do you'll not forget or be okay with what happened. But you'll give your heart permission to heal."

The words shook her to the core. A single tear rolled down her cheek.

"Prayer, sweetie. God can do amazing things, but if you choose to hold on to the pain, it only hurts you." He leaned down and kissed her head.

Words escaped her.

Gramps paused at the doorway. "By the way, I like Caleb. You can trust him."

His words only added to her turmoil. In the tumult she was going through, Caleb seemed to be an anchoring force. And she often found herself thinking of him, wondering what he'd think of this or that. The man had crept into her consciousness and burrowed himself into her heart.

Caleb woke with a jerk. The dream had been of his mother, brother and him standing around his father's grave, his mother crying, leaning on Sawyer. Kaye had been there, strong and silent, looking at him.

He took several deep breaths and swung his legs over the side of the bunk, running his hands through his hair. He slipped on his jeans and running shoes, opened the door to his trailer and sat on the steps.

Maybe it was seeing Kaye losing it this afternoon over her mother's things. He felt her pain. He hadn't felt that connection with another woman, and it scared him. Love. A lot was said about it, sung about it, written about it. But he hadn't seen what he considered the kind of love that the Bible talks about.

Caleb knew Kaye struggled with what happened to her and with her parents' deaths, but she didn't put it on display for others. She'd snapped out of her grief this afternoon before anyone could say anything and went on.

The soft breeze blew over his skin, much like a soothing hand of God.

Caleb walked into the barn and moved to the stall housing Razor. He stood there watching his horse sleep. After Sawyer, Razor was his best friend. They'd been through a lot of rodeos and had traveled the roads all over the West together.

Razor woke and turned to Caleb.

"Hey, fellow. I didn't mean to wake you." Caleb ran his hands over the horse's neck. "But I needed an old friend to talk to." The smoothness and warmth of Razor's coat brought comfort to his heart. He sat on the stool in front of Razor's stall.

When he'd talked to Joel earlier, that was the first time he'd told anyone about his secret desire to buy a ranch. What would it be like to wake up every day in the same place, to be surrounded by a wife and children? Was that possible for him?

Caleb knew he didn't want a woman like his mom. She couldn't make a decision without a man's input. After their dad had died, she'd changed into someone he didn't recognize. She'd gone from consulting Sawyer and him to pinning her hopes and decisions on her boyfriends—lots of boyfriends. She'd become needy and had deliberately turned a blind eye to the abuse her boyfriends had heaped on her sons.

A couple of the ladies he'd met in the rodeo had echoes of his mother, and he'd wanted nothing to do with them. He wanted a woman who could stand on her own. Kaye fell into that category, but she had her own problems plaguing her and probably didn't want to work sunup to sundown building a ranch. She hadn't stayed here.

But she was running. Joel had told him that.

Razor leaned over the half door of the stall and nipped his hair. "And you like Kaye, too, don't you, boy?" He reached up and patted the horse's neck. "You have any other input?"

Razor nodded his head.

"That doesn't help." Caleb shook his head. So much was in flux. His life was uncertain as of this moment. Kaye thought she might go for a counseling certificate, but her life was in as much chaos as his.

"Lord, I need some direction here."

He walked out of the barn to his trailer. The moon low on the horizon shone through some thin cirrus clouds, creating a ring around it. A prayer rose to his lips, and he prayed for Kaye. And he prayed for his mother. She no longer answered her sons' calls, and she'd moved away with one of her boyfriends to parts unknown. Neither he nor Sawyer knew where their mother was or how to contact her.

"Lord, I don't know where my mom is, but You do. Surround her with Your grace."

He walked back to his trailer, slipped off his shoes and jeans and climbed back into bed. Tomorrow he'd make a list of the things he needed to do to organize his part of the rodeo. Talking to Jack Murphy about providing the stock was priority number one. He came up with a list of eight other things, but the last thing that floated through his mind was how blue Kaye's eyes were.

He was for sure in trouble.

Chapter Seven

When Joel, Caleb and Kaye arrived home after another rodeo meeting the next day, the rest of the work on the house had been completed.

Gramps walked out on the porch. "It's all done. We have a porch roof, and there are new outlets in the bathroom."

Kaye held up the sack of food from the new barbecue restaurant in town. "We brought dinner." Exhausted from the day's meeting, they'd opted to pick up dinner instead of taking advantage of the new kitchen. They filed into the kitchen and worked together to get the meal on the table.

"How'd the meeting go?" Gramps asked, snatching a piece of fried okra.

"Everything's on track, Gramps," Kaye answered.

"We have six entrants in each event and decided to add a round of 'pin the calf' between the judges and county workers. The mayor, who invited himself to the meeting, liked the idea," Joel added.

Gramps stole another piece of fried okra. Kaye started to complain but caught Caleb joining Gramps in snatching some okra.

They settled down to eat.

After the blessing, Gramps said, "So Asa's going to be

chasing a calf around the infield of the stadium? That's enough to have the entire county buy tickets to see that spectacle. The man's too old to be acting like a teenager."

Kaye choked on a piece of roll. Her gaze flew to Caleb's. He hid his grin behind his coffee. Joel shrugged.

Gramps's bruises were fading nicely. His face held a sickly yellow tinge, the last color a bruise turns before it heals. He wore his sling tonight, and she wondered if he had been doing things today, using his arm in ways he shouldn't have. "Did I see apple pie?" Gramps asked.

"Nan brought apple pie to the board meeting," Kaye explained.

"You mean she brought apple pies for each member of the board?" Gramps looked around. Joel found the pieces of barbecue on his plate interesting.

Kaye and Caleb exchanged grins. Nan had caught Joel after the meeting and given him the pie. The look on her brother's face was priceless.

Kaye gathered up her grandfather's plate and put it in the dishwasher.

"Nan sure knows how to bake," Caleb teased.

"Then you court her," Joel shot back.

"I would, but she ignored me. She only had eyes for you."

"That's true, Joel." Kaye snickered.

Joel scowled.

"I'll say this about Nan." Kaye was enjoying herself. "She's got all those booths organized. And I can't believe how the rodeo's caught on. Why, it's spreading like wildfire."

"Laurie was responsible for that. She's got the thing all over the internet and Facebook. I wouldn't have thought of that." Joel took the last bite of his pie. After he swallowed, he licked the fork.

"You sure you don't want to reconsider Nan?" Caleb asked.

Joel didn't take the joke well. "Why don't we discuss the trip to Fort Worth tomorrow? Sis can drop us off at the coliseum and we can look at the stock, then she can do her errands and pick up what she needs for the rodeo."

"I also want to go by the college."

The men at the table looked at her. "What are you thinking, Sis?"

"Yeah, I want to know, too," Gramps added.

She explained about getting her counseling certification.

Gramps grinned. "I think you've got a Jim Dandy idea. You know my friend Marvin? His grandson came back from Afghanistan and isn't doing well. He's drinking and Marvin doesn't know what to do. When we came back from Korea, there were a few guys who had problems, but it wasn't talked about. It was swept under the rug. But now it seems our soldiers are suffering and we can't let them down. I'd be proud to have you helping those men and women."

She looked at her brother and Caleb. Both echoed Gramps's attitude. Caleb's expression particularly touched her. He knew about her flashback, but his attitude seemed to be *go for it*.

"So once we do morning chores, why don't we drive into Fort Worth after we have breakfast in Peaster to check in with folks and make sure they don't need anything?"

"You could call them on your cell," Kaye offered.

Joel gave her a long look. "Obviously, Sis, you've been away too long. Cowboys prefer face-to-face."

"The new phones have—"

"Trust me. It will be better if we do it in person. I might be able to convince a couple folks to help."

"Who?"

Joel just grinned like a Cheshire cat. "You'll just have to wait and see."

That wasn't her area of expertise.

The next morning, after they finished breakfast at the Country Kitchen Café, Joel, Gramps and Kaye went to talk to the mayor while Caleb walked to the feed store the next street over from the café. The old building, built in the fifties, had a big warehouse behind the front office.

"Morning," the owner called out.

"Hey, Ron."

"Joel need something for the ranch?"

Caleb knew all the shopkeepers in town. With his frequent visits to Peaster and Joel's introducing him around, he'd come to think of this town as his second home. "Nope. I wanted to talk to you about maybe helping the stock supplier who is providing the animals for the rodeo. I was wondering if you could work something out with your suppliers to donate some of what he'll need."

Ron rubbed his chin as he considered the request. "I like that idea. I'm thinking my suppliers might go for that. 'Course, they might want to use it in some publicity. That a problem?"

"No, and I'm sure Kaye will credit the companies who help out. And I'll be happy to defray any expenses you have." Caleb didn't like the idea of Ron being out a lot of money. They were all struggling at this point.

"My thanks. Let's see what we can do."

"Deal." Caleb offered his hand.

Ron shook it. "I'll say that having Joel's sister home, well, she's gotten this thing together, hasn't she?"

"Yeah, Kaye's something."

"Kaye?"

"I think she got used to going by her last name in the army, so she told me she wants to use Kaye."

Ron nodded. "I can understand that. It shocked this whole town when that drunk driver hit her folks head-on, killing her mom, dad and grandma. Br—Kaye and her grandfather were in the car following and saw everything.

"That accident changed her. I was in her class, and when she came back to school, she was a different girl, remote, like she was in another world. She never laughed or cracked a smile the rest of our senior year. She didn't bother with senior prom, and the morning after we graduated, when the rest of us were just waking up from all the parties, she was at the recruiter's office in Fort Worth, signing up. I don't know when she left for basic training, but we didn't see her after graduation. I never thought she'd come home."

"Sometimes our lives take unexpected turns." Caleb knew firsthand.

"I'm glad she's home and organizing this rodeo."

The bell on the shop rang and Kaye stepped in. "Hey, Ron," Kaye called out.

The man lit up. "Welcome home."

"Thank you. Caleb, Joel is in the truck with the motor running and you know how my brother is."

With a quick goodbye, they raced to the truck. As they drove into Fort Worth, Ron's words rolled around in Caleb's head. Joel had shared some details of what it was like when he came home after the accident, but Ron had colored the full picture for him. Caleb understood how it was to leave the old behind and begin anew.

As he learned more about Kaye, he discovered echoes of his life in hers, finding common ground. And new feelings started sprouting everywhere he turned. But he knew they were useless because there were too many hurdles in both his and Kaye's lives to hope for anything between them but friendship. But hope sometimes doesn't know hurdles.

"You be careful with my truck, Sis." Joel leaned in the driver's-side window, shaking his finger at her.

"You best ought to pull that finger back unless you'd like it broken." Men and their trucks. "I've driven a tank and a two-and-a-half ton cargo truck and a Humvee, so your *little* truck will not be a problem."

Gramps and Caleb snickered behind Joel. Out of the corner of her eye, Kaye saw Caleb grinning. When Joel turned around, the humor on Caleb's face disappeared.

"Well, those were the army's, but this is my baby." He tried to be stern but sounded like an eight-year-old warning another kid not to mess with his toy truck. "And you've been known not to be too careful with my things."

"Wow, who would've thought you carried around that incident with your good shirt for all these years. I was twelve." She threw a grin over his shoulder at her grandfather. "I promise to be careful with your baby."

Joel didn't look convinced.

"Chill out." She blew her brother a kiss and put the truck in gear and drove off.

It amazed her how healing just seeing the city of Fort Worth was. The trees were budding out in fresh green and the city had planted tulip bulbs and crocus in the median. A thousand shades of green surrounded her, so unlike the landscape of Iraq.

Cowboys. Cows. Horses. Home.

The familiar seemed to say *remember me?* She did, but could it be the way it was years ago?

No. Too many things had happened, but could she live here with the wounds and scars she now carried, inside and out? She wouldn't be wearing shorts anytime soon. Ugly, puckered scars crisscrossed her legs and abdomen.

The drive to the university only took her ten minutes. As she found a place to park, she prayed that God would guide her. She wasn't sure this was what she wanted to do, but it was the first step on the journey.

She'd gone online to check out the program the university offered and learned the name of the woman in charge of the certification. She found her office in one of the older buildings on campus. The plaque on the door said Tina Linton. A pretty blonde sat behind a beat-up desk. Kaye knocked on the door frame.

The woman looked up. "May I help you?"

"I was looking for Ms. Linton. I wanted to talk about what it would take to get my counseling certificate."

The woman leaned back in her chair. "Well, you're at the right place. I'm Tina Linton. What kind of counseling do you want to do, and what sort of degree do you already have?"

"I want to counsel soldiers coming back from Iraq and Afghanistan and help them readjust to life as a civilian."

"What qualifications do you have thus far so I can steer you in the right direction?" Tina asked.

"Well, I have a double major in social work/psychology and business."

"Once we get your transcripts I'll know better what you need, but what makes you want to go into that specialized field?"

"I'm an ex-soldier who has spent the last year in the hospital recovering from the wounds I suffered when a suicide bomber blew himself up in the café where I was meeting some local women."

"Come in. Let's talk."

* * *

Caleb sat next to Joel and Gramps, watching the horses they brought in for the auction.

"You like that mare?" Joel pointed to the mare in the ring.

The chestnut's coat glowed with health, and she had white stockings on her rear legs.

"She's good-looking."

The bidding started. Caleb debated with himself if now was the time to start investing in other horses. Razor would probably get along with her.

"Sold."

Gramps leaned over and in a loud whisper, he said, "You're a little slow, son. You know, if you don't make up your mind with women, they're gone before you know it. Other men move in and leave you flat-footed."

Caleb's eyes widened. Did Gramps mean more than the horse leaving the auction ring? Gramps's eyebrow arched and Caleb understood the man's words had more than one meaning.

"That was our last horse, and now we'll go on to the prize bulls," the announcer informed the audience.

The three men got up and walked out of the stands.

"I wonder if Sis has finished at the university." Joel led the way to the concessions outside the arena. They had just ordered some drinks when Kaye walked through the main doors to the coliseum.

She saw them, smiled and waved, heading over.

"Joel Kaye," a man's deep voice called out. "It seems like forever since I saw you. Joshua was marching around Jericho, if I recall." The men turned and saw a tall man walking toward them. "And Caleb Jensen. What are you doing here, you old dog? Aren't you still working the rodeo?"

"Reverend Charlie. How are you?" Caleb stepped up and shook Charlie's hand. Six feet plus with a full head of white hair and a rugged face that would've gone well in a Western movie, Charlie was a force to be reckoned with on the rodeo circuit. He didn't mince words, but the man would give you the shirt off his back, which Caleb had seen him do one day for a homeless man. "Well, we're here looking at stock for Joel."

Kaye joined the group and introductions were made.

"So you know my brother and Caleb?" she asked.

"I do, and I kept careful watch over their souls while they were on the circuit. I'll say they weren't my concern," the Reverend Charlie said.

"And how much did you pay him for that?" Kaye asked.

Before either man could react, the Reverend Charlie smiled and patted Caleb on the back. "No money changed hands. If I had a problem, they were first to come to my aid."

"What are you doing here, Charlie?" Caleb asked.

"I'm here to do a service in the stockyards tomorrow. Why don't y'all come? I've got a young man who is a great guitar player. And I'll know someone will be there for the service."

Caleb looked at the group. Kaye smiled. "I'd like that. I've heard how popular the cowboy church is getting, but I've never attended a service. I'd love to go. I'm sure our regular pastor won't mind. And it would be an honor to have you out at the ranch for lunch afterward. Maybe you can help us with ideas for our charity rodeo."

"Well, I certainly can't refuse such a wonderful invite. The service will be at eleven on Sunday down in the middle of the stockyards. There'll be signs."

"Then we'll see you Sunday."

Reverend Charlie nodded and walked out of the building.

"I've notified the people here and they're ready to talk to us about the charity rodeo."

"Then let's go."

Forty minutes later, they emerged from the business office. The staff confirmed they were on the right road and offered any help they needed.

"Since we're here, let's eat at Joe T. Garcia's for a late lunch. I mean, I've been home close to a week, and I've not had a meal at Joe T's."

The trip to the restaurant only took minutes. The lunch rush looked over since they could find a place to park. As they approached the door, a group came out, a couple and another man.

Kaye stopped, causing Caleb to run into her back. He wrapped his arms around her waist to keep her from falling. The man, whose arm was around the woman, looked up and missed a step. The woman collided with him.

Their companion kept going for a step, then paused.

The willowy blonde tugged on her date's arm. "Richard, honey, what's the—"

Richard gave her a chilling look. She stopped midsentence and looked at the people on the walk before her.

Joel and Gramps came up behind Kaye. Caleb didn't release Kaye and felt every muscle in her body stiffen. "Kaye?"

She smiled at him, but the tension in her body denied the smile.

Who was this guy? Caleb wondered as he watched the poisonous looks Joel and the unknown man exchanged.

The stranger's gaze took in Kaye from her head to foot, stopping at Caleb's arm around her waist. "You're not in uniform."

Kaye's shoulders stiffened. "It's nice to see you, too,

Richard." She held out her hand to the woman. "I'm Kaye. And you are?"

"I'm Ashley." The blonde raised her hand, but Richard's face darkened with anger. She didn't take Kaye's hand.

"She's not interested in you, Ash. She's just a jealous ex-wife knowing that I've moved on since our divorce," Richard snapped.

The girl paled.

This was Kaye's ex-husband? The instant the man had opened his mouth and insulted Kaye, Caleb was ready to set him straight. What had she seen in him? From Kaye's reaction, she wasn't too thrilled to see him now.

Kaye let her hand fall to her side.

Richard's hand clamped around Ashley's arm and started to pull her away.

"Ouch, you're hurting me."

"I see you haven't changed, Richard. I'm just sorry so many young women have to find out about you the hard way."

Richard took a step toward Kaye, then realized he was badly outnumbered. He grabbed Ashley's arm and pulled her toward a car. "You were never worth it."

Caleb felt Kaye's tremors, but she stood proudly and her silence was a bigger rebuke. Richard strode off. Ashley looked over her shoulder, her eyes soft with understanding.

"I never liked him," Gramps grumbled. "What you saw in that man, I'll never know."

"You know, Gramps, I wonder the very same thing. Momentary insanity?"

Caleb released Kaye and they headed into the restaurant. After they were seated and ordered their meal, Gramps patted Kaye's hand. "I'm glad that man is no longer in your life, and if my arm wasn't in a sling— Well,

I've wrestled some ornery steers, and he wouldn't have been a problem."

"How did your meeting at the university go?" Caleb asked, wanting to get Kaye's mind on something else.

The muscles in her shoulders eased. "The director of the program told me the different directions I could go and asked what level of counseling I wanted to do. But she was very supportive and gave me a contact at the VA where they need some volunteer help. She also told me about a private group of ex-military doctors and nurses working with veterans."

Kaye's face changed from troubled to excited as she talked about helping other veterans. Caleb wondered how she could've married so obnoxious a man as they just met.

She dipped a tortilla chip into the salsa the waiter set on the table. "So did you find any horses you wanted to buy?"

Her question jerked Caleb back to the conversation flowing around the table. "I saw a mare I was tempted to buy, but I need to find a place before I can buy another horse. Razor might be offended if he had to share his trailer, and I know he's not willing to do that, even if my trailer would hold a second horse."

"Is that what was stopping you?" Joel frowned. "You could've kept that mare at the ranch. Had I known…" He shook his head.

Before anyone could comment, the waiter arrived with lunch and all thoughts turned to food. As Caleb ate his chili relleno, he caught a hint of sadness in Kaye's blue eyes, but when she turned to him, she hid the pain and tried to gloss over her emotions.

Here was another example of how Kaye didn't allow circumstances to beat her, but she fought back. Not one word of pity or poor me, but then any woman who'd made it to the rank of captain couldn't be a clinging vine. Kaye was a woman who battled the odds and stood on her own.

Her ex's behavior left a bad taste in his mouth, much like eating dirt when you fell off a horse. He was surprised Joel hadn't punched out the man. He'd certainly asked for it. But Kaye had kept her cool, which he admired. Thinking back to the exchange outside the restaurant, something bothered him about it other than the obvious. But what? What was going on?

Kaye caught his eye again, and he felt a connection to her. He didn't know what this feeling was, but wanted to explore it.

Chapter Eight

After a late evening meal of sandwiches and fresh chocolate-chip cookies that Nan White had dropped off, Joel stood. "I'm going to do evening chores."

Kaye caught him before he escaped out the back door. "Nope. You need to make calls for the charity rodeo that you haven't done yet. I'll do the chores."

Joel opened his mouth to protest, but she rested her hands on her hips. "Are you going to keep your word?"

Brother and sister stared at each other. "You hit below the belt."

She didn't move.

Sighing, Joel walked into the dining room.

Caleb laughed as he and Kaye walked to the barn. "You certainly know how to pull Joel's chain. When Nan showed up earlier with those cookies, he looked ready to bolt like a trapped cow unwilling to be branded."

"But she's done a good job with her part, which is more than Joel's done."

They divided the chores and went to work.

After mucking out the last stall, Kaye put out fresh hay for Midnight. "I did miss this."

Caleb stopped and looked up. "Mucking out stalls?"

"Oddly enough, yes. I missed working with horses. Somehow, it connected me with the past." In a safe way. Only good memories were attached with horses. "I rode while in the service, but working with the animals, caring for them, I didn't get to do that. There's something so soothing about the smell of a horse and the warmth of their body." When she was in basic, she'd put all her grief and sorrow in the daily chores and routine. The chaplain had noticed her intensity and had asked what was bothering her. His observation had caught her by surprise.

Caleb walked to the stall where she was working. "Yeah, I have good memories of working with my dad in the barn."

He leaned against the stall. "Sawyer and I were probably not much of a help for our dad, but it was great to listen to him tell stories about when he grew up." He rubbed the back of his neck.

She put up the pitchfork. "I remember following my dad out here. I wanted to help him in the barn instead of helping my mom do dishes. My mom was frustrated that I didn't want to be in the kitchen with her when I was a little girl. She wondered if I missed the girl gene. I know I missed the housework gene." She laughed and rested her arms on the top rail of the stall, remembering her mom's allowing her the freedom to work with her dad.

"You okay?" Caleb asked, looking into her face.

"I am. Sometimes memories can bring a smile, unlike the bad ones we ran into at Joe T's." She noticed no one had mentioned her ex's rude behavior at the restaurant.

"No kidding."

He said it in such a deadpan way, she laughed.

He stepped closer, leaning on the stall wall. "I thought your brother was going to punch out that man, and if he wasn't, I was tempted. Was he always that much of a jerk?"

Kaye hadn't noticed. She'd been too busy trying to hold on to her temper. "No, the man could be charming."

Caleb gave her a look that said he didn't believe her.

"Really. It was only at the end of our marriage when he tried to provoke a reaction out of me. He changed once the band started achieving some success. He claimed I didn't share his dream, but his dream only bled us of money instead of adding to it. Being practical, I wanted to eat."

Caleb reached out and took her hand. "Hey, don't downplay that. Eating has a lot going for it." He grinned and she knew he understood at a gut level.

She wondered what had possessed her to marry Richard in the first place, a musician who lived moment to moment.

It must've been temporary madness. They'd eloped and she'd brought him home once. "The only time he came home with me was the Christmas after we married, and neither Joel nor Gramps liked him. Richard returned the sentiment."

"I can see why they didn't like him."

Her head came up, ready to challenge him. "It was that obvious, wasn't it?"

"Plain as the tail on my horse."

A grin split her face. "Yeah, well, who can account for chemistry? Makes me kinda leery to trust those feelings again. You end up doing stupid stuff." She remembered the ugly argument she'd had with Richard the last time they were together. He'd called her a repressed old army hag who had no imagination or creativity and only knew how to follow the rules, and then he'd stormed out of the house.

"It looks like your ex hasn't changed."

Caleb didn't offer any criticism of her erratic behavior. She wasn't so kind to herself. She beat herself up for her poor judgment. "I feel sorry for that young woman. I don't think she'll leave the relationship whole." She wanted to snatch her words back. What was it about this man that had her confessing all her weaknesses? He had to think of her as a head case.

Embarrassed she'd revealed so much, she headed outside to bring Midnight into the barn. She waved a carrot at Midnight but got Razor instead.

"You, I don't need." Razor took the carrot. Suddenly, she felt Caleb's warmth behind her and he waved a carrot at Midnight. She came trotting up to the fence and took the carrot.

Caleb caught Razor's halter and led him inside. Midnight followed. Kaye took the horse into her stall and picked up the curry brush. She wanted the comfort of the mare's warmth to settle into her soul, but instead she got Caleb's understanding.

"I'll see you tomorrow," Caleb said and left the barn.

As she worked on brushing her mare, Kaye lost herself in prayer. Seeing Richard was like a poke in the eye. "Lord, I don't understand why it still hurts so bad. Why?"

She stopped and rested her head against Midnight's side.

Midnight's head turned toward Kaye. Kaye blinked away the moisture. "I love you, too." Kaye kissed Midnight between her eyes. "Thanks, girl, for listening."

As she walked inside, she pushed aside the hurt. Tears would gain her nothing. She'd lost that strong Captain Brenda who faced down the enemy, driving a truck through insurgent fire. Where was that woman?

She thought about that carrot that had appeared before her face and the man who'd thought to bring it and help her bring the horses in. He was the first man—aside from her family—who'd acted so thoughtfully toward her. It awed her and touched a heart she'd thought hardened. Maybe there was more than one reason God had brought her home.

* * *

Sunday morning, after the stock was cared for and a quick breakfast, they started out for Fort Worth. Caleb and Kaye rode in the backseat. The absurd idea of grabbing Kaye's hand flashed through Caleb's brain. It was just lack of sleep, he told himself. But thoughts of Kaye kept flashing through his brain when he closed his eyes. The shock of meeting her ex-husband had thrown Caleb off balance. Kaye seemed such a determined woman that he couldn't see how she fell for such a con artist.

Of course, matters of the heart were still a mystery. Wasn't that what was said in Proverbs? Who can understand the way of a man with a maid? Well, Caleb had to agree with Solomon; this falling-in-love business was beyond understanding. When Sawyer and he ended up living at the apartment in back of the church in Plainview, he'd asked Pastor Garvey about love, because the episodic thing his mother experienced couldn't be love.

Pastor told them love was an action, determination not feeling. When Sawyer and he had given the pastor a blank look, he'd encouraged them to watch his congregation. And watch they had. What they'd seen had amazed them— husbands caring for their wives and children, mothers sacrificing so their sons or daughters could compete in 4-H and travel to be in the finals. Or a father, one of the church elders, using the money he'd saved for a new truck to pay for his daughter's last year of beauty school. They'd seen and understood what the pastor had been talking about.

Caleb had never seen such action before, but the pastor's words took on skin and bone.

Was that the reason he felt so drawn to Kaye? Her actions proved her heart? Or was it that she was in the middle of transition, the same as he, two souls at a crossroad? Was that why he understood her so well? When he'd held her in the thunderstorm, he'd felt her pain. She hadn't had to explain anything afterward. He'd known. She touched something deep inside him. Both of their paths were uncertain, but more than that, his confidence in himself had been shaken. He was the man everyone depended on from the time he could remember. With the accident, that belief in himself had been shaken.

The Fort Worth stockyards came into view. Kaye looked around the corrals. "I'm interested in seeing this cowboy church. I've heard that this is taking off in different places."

"What happens when it rains?" Gramps asked.

"I guess they scatter for shelter," Joel answered.

"Well, I know a couple cowboy churches where they have a corrugated roof and open sides," Caleb explained. "I've seen several on country roads outside Midland and Abilene."

"Well, we shouldn't have any problems today," Kaye added.

The morning couldn't have been more perfect. The sky was a bright blue and the temperature was in the low 70s. Trees had new shoots on them, and the leaves that had appeared were a light green. A gentle breeze blew through the window.

They pulled into a parking lot, filling with trucks. A small sign the size of a For Sale sign announced Cowboy Church services, 10:30 p.m. Charlie Newman, Preaching.

"I think we've found the right place." Gramps surveyed the parking lot. "At least we're not going to be the only ones here. It would've been embarrassing, but of course, I've been to services when I was just a whippersnapper when it was only a handful of folks—my parents, brothers and sisters and the neighboring family."

Caleb also wondered how many people would be here.

The small number he'd expected turned out to be closer to seventy.

"Did you think we were going to be the only ones attending, Gramps?" Kaye asked as she followed him out of the truck.

Gramps harrumphed.

As they filed into the roped-off area, several cowboys nodded to them or tipped their hats. Kaye seemed to be the recipient of several hat tips.

"Ma'am."

"I almost feel like I'm back in the service with all these ma'ams," she whispered to Caleb.

"Caleb Jensen," a man called out. A cowboy with bowed legs slipped out of a group clustered at the front of the area. He wore a white Western shirt, pressed jeans with creases, big belt buckle and boots. Mack Lodge grasped Caleb's hand and vigorously shook it. Mack had been on the circuit for the past couple years. The kid was an eager worker, who saw his time in rodeo as a stepping-stone to owning his own spread. "It's good to see you, friend. We've been missing you on the circuit, and everyone is asking when you're coming back. And the other pick-up guys are missing ya, too."

Mack's well-meaning words were a knife in his gut, only adding to his self-doubt. He tried to smile but didn't know if he pulled it off. "It's good to see you, too, Mack. I've been taking a little time off to help a friend, Joel Kaye." Introductions were made.

Mack tipped his hat to Kaye. "I hope you haven't been on the mean side of Caleb's horse. That horse is a good athlete, but cantankerous, and I've sported the bruises to prove it."

Caleb gave Kaye a "see, I told you so" look.

"Razor and I have become good friends."

Mack's jaw went slack. He turned to Caleb. "She's joshing me, right?"

"No. It knocked me back on my boots, too, Mack."

"It's a pleasure, ma'am, to meet you. No one will believe that story." He backed away. "Well, hurry back, Caleb. The guy they've got riding now isn't as good as you."

Caleb nodded but knew the accident was the talk of the circuit.

Mack hesitated then added, "No one blames you for what happened. It was just one of those things."

Caleb's heart jerked. "Thanks."

Caleb felt Kaye at his arm. When he looked down, she smiled her reassurance.

A guitar started playing the song "Awesome God." People slipped into different rows and joined in singing. Caleb followed Kaye into a row of seats. The guitarist played a couple more songs, leading the crowd in the chorus, ending with "Turn Your Eyes Upon Jesus." After the final chord died, the Reverend Newman stepped up to the lectern.

"Welcome, folks, to our service. I see some new faces and I want you to turn and greet the person next to you, welcoming them. If you don't know your neighbor, you'll meet some new friends."

The cowboys and cowgirls turned to each other. There were only a couple people who Caleb didn't know, but all his old friends shook his hand and told him they missed him. Their welcomes and encouragement pushed him into further turmoil. He was missed, but his guilt ate a hole in his gut. Nothing had been settled in the weeks he'd been at Joel's ranch.

They sat back into the folding chairs and Charlie started his sermon. "I'm glad you're here this morning. I wanted to share with you what God laid on my heart.

"You remember how Peter pledged to fight for Christ

to the death, but when Peter was put to the test, he failed, denying Christ. Not once, but three times. You can maybe understand once, but three times?

"Don't you think if Jesus hadn't confronted Peter after the resurrection, then maybe Peter's guilt would've crippled him after Christ ascended?"

As Charlie continued his message, Caleb felt the words hit him in the chest. "Peter's not unique. We've all failed Christ. But does He hold it against us? No. After you've failed once, you think God's going to throw you out? Peter repented and look what he accomplished after he knew he was forgiven."

Each word Charlie spoke added to Caleb's discomfort. He glanced at Kaye. Charlie's words were finding their mark there, too.

Charlie continued his sermon about forgiving one another but that we don't include ourselves in that forgiveness. "Folks, you need to surrender to God those fears and mistakes that are tying you up. If you try to bury them, act like nothin's wrong, you'll simply have to deal with them later when you dig them up, and face them.

"Why not just give God that guilt, anger or problem now? He will guide you through the storm and help you come out on the other side. And if you think He doesn't know, then you're wrong.

"So why not give it up?"

Kaye squirmed in her chair. Caleb resisted the urge to move, but Charlie's words grabbed him, too.

"Let's end the service with the song 'Amazing Grace' and put those cares in His hands."

The guitar player strummed the first chords of the song.

Caleb knew God was dealing with him. Did God want his guilt? Was he hanging on to it?

The congregation started filing out of the rows, greeting each other. Caleb introduced Kaye and the others to his friends. Charlie joined them. "Hope you enjoyed the service."

"Ah, food for thought, Reverend," Gramps answered. "You stepped on a few toes."

Charlie smiled. "Good, that means God was working in those words."

"Reverend Charlie, you still planning on coming to the ranch for lunch?" Joel asked. "I know my sister would like to pick your brain for ideas for the charity rodeo."

Charlie's face lit up. "I can't pass up a home-cooked meal."

"Well, it wasn't me that put in the roast. It was Joel. The army used to cook all my meals."

Charlie looked from Kaye to Joel. "Who's to say men can't cook? Not many women were cooks on cattle drives. Chuck wagons were known for their male cooks."

Frowning, Joel looked around. "I don't know if that's a compliment or insult."

"Depends on your skill," Charlie answered. "After we put up the chairs, I can join you and follow you out to your ranch."

"Well, Charlie," Gramps said, "if we all pitch in, we'll eat sooner."

"I like how you think, Niall Kaye, but let the youngsters do the work."

Caleb was amazed that Charlie knew Gramps's given name. Very few people called him Niall.

They all went to work putting the chairs on the cart. Within five minutes, all signs of the service were gone and the chairs were returned to the storeroom.

"I'm ready to eat," Charlie announced. "You lead the way and I'll follow."

As they drove back to Peaster, Charlie's sermon rumbled around Caleb's head.

Kaye leaned close and whispered, "Are you okay?"

Wow, how the tables had turned. "Why do you ask?"

"Because you look like I did when I ran into my ex."

Chapter Nine

"Why don't we eat out on the newly rebuilt porch and enjoy Joel's and Caleb's handiwork?" Kaye suggested. "We won't have many days like this, so let's take advantage of it."

The guys gave her a puzzled look.

"There's no furniture out there, Sis. How we going to do that? Sit cross-legged on the ground? I mean, I'm sure you did that in the army, but we've got a perfectly good table and chairs here in the kitchen and dining room."

The formal dining room table still held all the papers for the rodeo and the outside picnic table stood half charred. Kaye surveyed the group. "I have three strong cowboys here, minus Gramps, who should be able to move the kitchen table out onto the porch."

The men traded looks. Joel looked frustrated. Caleb's mouth turned into a smile.

"I like Kaye's suggestion," Charlie offered. "Let's enjoy the day the Lord has given us."

"She's right," Gramps added. "It's a nice spring afternoon. I think it's a good idea."

They easily moved the kitchen table and chairs out onto the porch. Kaye handed each man plates, silverware and glasses. The food dishes came next and, within five minutes, they sat down to Sunday dinner.

"Gramps, why don't you say the blessing?" Joel said.

He nodded and began, "Lord, thank You that we could gather around the bountiful table, and thank You that my grandchildren are home and we have guests. But we are most thankful that You have never forsaken us, no matter what has happened. Thank You for the bounty. Amen."

The prayer touched Kaye, and when she opened her eyes and saw the gathered people, she wished her mother, father and grandmother were here.

"Hand me the rolls, Sis." Joel's comment interrupted her thoughts.

"A man driven by his stomach." She gave him the basket of rolls.

They quickly passed around the dishes of food. "That was a good sermon you preached today, Charlie," Gramps said again.

Kaye stilled. Was Gramps trying to tell her something?

Charlie nodded. "It was something God's been dealing with me for some time. I talk to lots of cowboys out there on the circuit, and they turn their lives around, but they're haunted by things they did or that happened in the past." He forked a piece of meat into his mouth and chewed. "So they're toting a bale load of grief along with them on the circuit. Instead, I want to see them laughing with joy that God has redeemed them.

"I know when I was in my late teens, early twenties, I did my share of drinking and carousing. I ended up marrying a young lady and having twin girls." He fell silent for a moment. "I was off rodeoing in Arizona when my house back in Abilene caught fire."

Kaye's heart stopped, fearing what she'd hear next.

"They all died in that fire. My girls and wife." He paused.

Everyone at the table knew Charlie's grief.

"I was out on a bender for six months," Charlie quietly continued. "One day, I ended up in the graveyard sitting beside my family's graves. It must've been two in the morning, and I started yelling at God. How could He allow this to happen?

"Then I asked God why."

"You get an answer?" Caleb asked.

Charlie turned his head. "No, but I knew my sweet wife and babies were in heaven. You see, she'd started going to church and had wanted me to come with her and make peace with God. She'd just dedicated the girls to the Lord that Sunday. I told her I wasn't driving home for the service, since I was in the finals that Sunday afternoon."

Charlie's story struck a chord in Kaye's heart. Charlie had been running away from God. She understood only too well.

"Once I gave the Lord that anger, I began to heal. I was able to be quiet with myself. Does that make sense?" He looked around the table.

When he came to her, Kaye knew what her face would tell. "So is that when you started preaching?"

"I saw others who needed help. I went to seminary, but when I finished, I knew the cowboys on the circuit needed ministering to, so here I am, twenty-five years later."

"I never knew, Charlie," Caleb said, "about your family. I'm sorry."

"It's not something a lot of folks know, but Gramps asked where the sermon this morning came from. And who knows who was in the audience today that needed that truth. God knows."

Kaye's gaze met Caleb's. The air vibrated between them.

"So how are things on the rodeo circuit?" Caleb asked.

"It's going well. Mike Rogers is scoring big points with each rodeo going toward that world-championship belt buckle. He's proud as a peacock. There's been a couple bronc riders who've asked when you're coming back. They've got no complaints about the other guy, but you've got him beat hands down. The guys have confidence in you."

Caleb tried to hide his reaction, but Kaye noticed the tightening of his shoulders. "I appreciate that, Charlie. And I'm glad to hear Mike's closing in on that championship buckle."

Charlie's eyes narrowed and Kaye wondered if Charlie would challenge Caleb to talk about what was eating at him. She would guess it had something to do with the accident. What happened had to be hard to live with, but didn't Caleb realize things happen? He couldn't control everything.

"How's your brother?" Charlie asked. "Has he graduated yet?"

"He has. He got his masters last summer. He focused on business management, but his area was companies in trouble. He wanted to be a turn-around specialist focusing on rodeo and rodeo management."

Charlie grabbed the last roll. "I'm impressed."

Kaye was, too.

"It took Sawyer's professors a while to warm up to the idea, but when they thought about it, they realized those skills could be applied to traveling circuses or ice shows. Right now he's evaluating a rodeo in Tyler."

"So what are you going to do now?" Charlie pressed. "You going to continue rodeoing?"

"I'm thinking on it."

Charlie turned to Kaye. "You should've seen these two

when they were on the circuit. Sawyer, Caleb's younger brother, was a great rider. I think if he would've stayed with the rodeo, he could've had a championship belt buckle."

"I wanted Sawyer to have that degree. He can have a successful life that's not as hard on the body."

Charlie swallowed the last bite of his roll. "True, Caleb. And I think that was smart of you to direct your brother that way. And Sawyer credits his big brother with the push."

Kaye's heart found another reason to admire Caleb, and she realized that he'd been worming himself into her heart while she was trying to cope with the fallout here.

"You do what you have to," Caleb quietly answered.

For several moments, silence reigned, punctuated with the sounds of birds chirping and a cow mooing.

"You ready for cake?" Kaye asked. Nan had delivered it last night. If her brother didn't tell Nan he wasn't interested, she'd end up twenty pounds heavier.

Charlie brightened. "Homemade?"

"Yes." Kaye directed her look at her brother. He glanced away.

Kaye retrieved the cake and plates and quickly sliced pieces for everyone.

"Okay, tell me why you are doing this rodeo," Charlie began, "and how I can help."

Joel nodded toward Kaye. "Sis is running the show. What do you need?"

She explained about buying seed grain for the ranchers. "If you could get the word out about the rodeo to all your contacts, I'd appreciate it. Hopefully, we have people attending and ticket sales will help with expenses. And any cowboys who want to compete are welcome. If you'd like to come back and do the Sunday-morning service, that would be great. I think several of the local pastors might want to join in with you."

"I like that idea. I'd love to team up with the other local pastors and minister to the people here."

Things were coming together. "Thanks."

Charlie looked at his watch. "I need to go back into Fort Worth. I may be a preacher, but I take my horse with me. I have to get him."

They rose and gathered the dishes, carrying them into the kitchen. The men also moved the furniture back inside. Kaye listened to the men talk while Joel helped her load the dishwasher.

"Caleb," Charlie said in a quiet voice. "I want you to know Tag Johnson is doing fine. He's going to be released from the hospital next week."

Kaye strained to hear Caleb's response. Caleb said something, but she couldn't understand his words. She glanced over her shoulder. Caleb stood next to Charlie, their faces close together. Caleb's grim expression cut across her heart. The man hurt.

Joel touched her hand. "Sis."

She jerked around to face her brother. "What?"

He looked at the plate she held under the running water.

"Here." She handed him the plate.

"You shouldn't be snooping."

Kaye rinsed another dish. "I wasn't."

"For shame, fibbing while Charlie is right here in the kitchen."

"Has Caleb talked to you about what happened?"

"No, and I didn't ask."

Kaye understood the male culture of never talking about feelings. But she'd also known fellow soldiers and officers who suffered when they kept it inside. Wasn't that why she was going into counseling? "It doesn't go away," she whispered.

Joel looked down at her. "I know, Sis."

His words were colored with pain, and she couldn't figure out if it was his pain or if he was talking about hers.

Charlie walked to the sink. "I want to thank y'all for lunch. I'm going to do all I can to help. What are the dates?"

Kaye dried off her hands. "It will be Memorial Day weekend."

Reverend Charlie grabbed his cowboy hat and held it in his right hand. "I'll make sure I'm here."

"Wait, Charlie. I'll give you the email address where you can contact us and give it out to others." Kaye raced into the dining room and grabbed a handful of business cards the mayor had printed for the rodeo. "Here, spread them around."

"Good thinking, Kaye." Charlie tucked the cards into the front pocket of his Western shirt.

Joel slipped his arm around her and hugged. "She's a pro at this. That's why I convinced her to do it."

"Maybe I should have her schedule my services for me."

"Talk to me after the rodeo is over."

He nodded and walked out to his truck, waving as he pulled away.

"Well, I think I'm going to check to make sure there are no cows down in the stream," Caleb said. He turned and walked to the barn.

"You think you should help him?" Kaye asked her brother.

He frowned at her. "No."

"Okay."

"You're not going to argue?"

"No. I understand the man needs his space." She turned

and walked inside. She might need a long ride this afternoon herself, for there were lots of things rolling around inside, and she needed some time and space to deal with them.

She also needed to talk to God.

Caleb rode like the hounds of hell were after him. If he could ride fast enough, maybe he could leave behind the truth Charlie had told him.

Tag would soon be released from the hospital. He was in a body cast and would stay that way for a couple more weeks. How was the man going to provide for his family?

The incident haunted Caleb, sitting on his shoulder like a vulture, ready to swoop down and pick the bones of his carcass clean. This was the first time he'd doubted his skill in the ring.

He rode down to the stand of trees where he'd held Kaye while she'd relived her nightmare. Dismounting Razor, he walked to one of the trees and sat, using the trunk as a backrest.

"Lord, what am I going to do? How can I make my failure right?"

He rested his head on the trunk and stayed quiet. The pain he'd been keeping at bay slammed into him. He'd failed. He'd failed Tag, letting him be injured. He'd failed to protect his brother from his mom's boyfriend's abuse. He'd failed his mom—never being able to make things just right so she could function. The order he'd thought he'd built in his world had shattered the night of Tag's accident, leaving him among the rubble of his life. "Oh, Lord, what am I to do now? I no longer know who I am."

There were no words for his pain, no tears, just the soul-deep ache that he couldn't outrun, no matter how hard he tried. Charlie's reassurance that Tag was doing okay hit

Caleb hard. He relived those terrifying twelve seconds when he'd held Tag's life in his hands. Surely he could've done something else.

Time ceased to matter and only after Razor walked to where he sat and nudged Caleb with his nose, did he move. "Stop."

Razor didn't pay attention. He nudged Caleb again.

"What?" Caleb looked up and saw the sun had moved in the sky just above the Western horizon. Amazed that he'd been here that long, he stood, mounted Razor and started to the house, knowing he hadn't settled anything yet, but God was dealing with the pain he tried to bury. Charlie's sermon had grabbed his heart and forced him to deal with the incident.

Kaye spent the afternoon going through her emails from the other members of the organizing committee. She was happy to learn that registration for the different events in the rodeo had risen, and they were filling up quickly.

"Are you working on Sunday?" Gramps asked as he walked into the room.

"I am."

"Back in my day, it was frowned upon to work on Sunday, with the exception of feeding your stock."

"So how'd that work, Gramps?" Kaye remembered her grandmother scolding her mother about ironing on Sunday.

"The way you did it was getting your work done on the other days." He sat at the table. Gramps's bruises were just about gone and he wasn't wearing the sling. "Your grandma did all her cooking on Saturday. Dishes stayed in the sink until Monday morning."

"But didn't she have to work twice as hard on Monday?"

"Indeed, but she could count on resting on Sunday. It was just the way it was done."

Kaye realized the fierce pain that always accompanied thoughts of her grandmother wasn't as intense. Being home made her confront the past.

"Charlie had a good sermon this morning."

The reason for Gramps's visit became clear. She eyed him. "It was good."

He studied her. "I'll tell you, at the oddest moments I miss your grandmother. When I see a baby lamb out in the field, or a sunset that sets the whole sky on fire, I think of her. Your grandmother loved to see those sunsets. Sometimes we'd sit on the porch and just thank the Lord He'd helped us through the day.

"Like Charlie says, you bury those hurts—they don't go away."

Gramps knew why she enlisted. That New Year's Eve tragedy overwhelmed her, and the army had given her a different focus, allowing her to push away all her baggage. But her heart still ached. With time and different locales, it'd been easier to bury that ache. Here, she found them again, and this time she needed to face them.

"I hear you."

He searched her face. "Pain like that, child, can't be left behind. It goes with you."

Gramps had hit it on the mark. Leaning forward, she kissed him on the cheek. "I know." Maybe that was why she'd overlooked so many of the warning signs that had been there with Richard.

Gramps leaned back and studied her. "Then make peace like the preacher told ya." He nodded, stood and left the room.

Added to those old wounds were the new ones she accumulated on the way—a broken marriage and the death of those Iraqi women. She took a deep breath. "I don't know how to handle all this, Lord."

As she stared at the listing of registrants for the rodeo, the names blurred. The air turned heavy, pressing in on her. She stood and raced outside, needing to be astride a horse. Her legs had grown stronger from her constant riding and the normal chores of a ranch. It was like a confirmation in her soul that she'd needed to come home.

She saddled Midnight, mounted and started riding. It didn't matter where, just being on top of a horse and galloping across the ranch land, feeling the freedom, brought her a brief reprieve.

She let the horse have her head and raced across the rolling prairie. How long they galloped, Kaye had no idea, but when she saw the stand of trees where Caleb and she had taken shelter, she pulled up on Midnight's reins. The horse slowed down. She passed the trees and headed for the river, hoping there was some water there for the horse to drink.

The rain had brought the stream up to a trickle and her horse drank.

She heard a horse behind her. Turning in the saddle, she saw Caleb and Razor coming toward them.

"What are you doing out here?" Kaye asked.

"I could ask the same question."

"Clearing my head." Maybe Charlie's sermon had touched Caleb, too. "It seems a lot of us are doing some thinking."

"That's the sign of some good preaching. The old timers called it conviction."

Kaye leaned on the saddle horn. "I know." She looked over at the stand of trees. Added to all the other memories she was fighting, this was where she'd flipped out.

"Would you like to walk our horses?" Caleb gently asked.

Midnight could use a walk after the hard run Kaye had put the mare through. "Sounds good."

They both dismounted and started walking along the creek bank. "Do you ever wonder why things happen?" What happened to the stoic officer who could deal with the chaos and demands of a company of soldiers? Or the demands of dozens of native civilians?

"I do."

"Being here, I've run into the teenage Brenda, who wonders why things happen. Why did my parents have to die? Why did my marriage fail so miserably? And why did I survive that bomb blast when the others didn't?"

Caleb stopped and faced her. "I think Charlie was right. We have to deal with stuff. Sometimes there is no explanation for what happens, but heaven knows the reason. We need to ask the Lord to help us come to peace with those things.

"As for your husband, well, he doesn't seem too bright."

A choked laugh escaped her.

"Sorry. That probably wasn't in the spirit of what Charlie would've said, but I know this—your husband was wrong."

Caleb's words settled into her heart as if God had sent His blessing on the ragged edges of her memories. She took a deep breath. "So were you dealing with your own problems?"

"Yeah, I was wrestling with some old wounds."

"Was it about the accident? I couldn't help but overhear what Charlie said to you."

He gave her a self-effacing grin. "Yeah, it was."

"Well, then, both of us have accidents that we need to face."

They continued walking. Swallowing hard, he opened his mouth then closed it. Finally, "You've heard several folks talking about Taggert Johnson?"

She glanced at him. "Yes, I've heard his name."

"Tag was the last rider of the night at the Albuquerque rodeo. He made his ride, but after the buzzer went off, he didn't release. It looked like his glove got caught under the grip and he couldn't get his hand loose. I rode close while the other pick-up man tried to block the horse, and I was able to grab Tag around the waist, but just as I was pulling him free, Mankiller turned hard to his flank and jerked Tag away. I lost my hold and he slipped in my grip. I didn't completely lose him, but he was just hanging in my arm, a perfect target for that horse. A couple kicks caught Tag's lower abdomen and legs. Mankiller caught me, too, on my upper arm, but I didn't drop him. The other pick-up man was able to grab the trailing reins of the horse and lead him away.

"Tag was in surgery that night to remove his spleen. He also was in traction for a while. He's still in the hospital."

The man's shoulders slumped and Kaye could see the weight of the guilt riding him hard.

"It sounds like an accident to me."

"You're not just saying that because you feel sorry for me?"

"Why would you think that?"

"To ease my guilt."

"No. I call them as I see them. I was never one to excuse bad behavior, but accidents happen. What happened sounds like something you had no control over." The words stopped her as their meaning sunk into her soul. "Kinda like a car wreck," she breathed.

Caleb watched her face. "Yeah, kinda like that."

Kaye realized that she had a lot of things in common with the man. She understood his pain. "I guess God sent us Charlie this morning to help us get things straight. Now, if only I can put into practice his message of letting it go and giving it to God."

He stepped closer to her and his tender expression made her knees weak. He took her chin between his thumb and forefinger and gently moved her face up. His lips covered hers. She allowed the tenderness of the kiss to wash over her. When he pulled back, she could see the warmth in his eyes.

Her cell phone rang.

Caleb nodded toward her phone. "I think that's probably your brother wondering where you are."

Kaye answered her phone.

"Hey, Sis. I've got Mike, Laurie and Nan here. They said you were supposed to have a meeting at the house at three-thirty."

Kaye looked down at her watch. She'd forgotten the meeting. "Tell them I'll be right there." She disconnected and looked at Caleb. "Rodeo board is at the house. We had a meeting this afternoon that should've started ten minutes ago."

"Then let's mount up and ride."

Kaye looked at the stirrup. Caleb stepped to her side and offered his locked fingers as an aid. She stepped into his hands and he lifted her up, then mounted his own horse.

"Thank you, Caleb." There was so much more she wanted to say to this man who'd helped her deal with her ghosts. "I'm going to get well enough to mount by myself."

He nodded, looking up at her. "Want to race?" The corner of his mouth kicked up.

She didn't bother to answer, but kicked Midnight into a run.

"Hey, that's not fair."

She laughed.

Chapter Ten

Caleb had thought he could escape the board meeting at the house. It didn't work out. Joel laughed at Caleb, but his laughter quickly died when Kaye nailed him, too.

Caleb listened as the members finished going over the lists.

"I think every church in town has a committee to help with the rodeo," Nan said. "I know several of the ladies at First Community have been talking it up at their workplaces in Fort Worth. Shirley Owens works with a law firm. She told several of the lawyers about it. They're going to talk to some of their clients about helping to sponsor events or just to contribute to the cause of buying seed for the ranchers."

Kaye smiled. "That's terrific."

"And I think Shirley might contact one of the local TV stations about doing a piece on the charity rodeo."

"That will get us some free publicity," Mike added. "It might add to some more cowboys registering for the rodeo, too."

The chatter continued.

Joel leaned over and whispered to Caleb, "You're smiling."

Caleb jerked his gaze to Joel. "What?"

"You're smiling. And when you and Sis raced up to the barn, she was laughing."

"So?"

"What's up?" Joel waited, his gaze penetrating.

"What do you think, Joel?" Kaye asked, breaking into their whispered conversation.

"Huh?"

"Do you think we need to pursue more sponsors? Nan thinks Shirley might get another law firm to help sponsor an event."

"Sounds good."

"Okay. Let's go with that." Kaye looked around the table. "Anything else?"

No one added anything.

"Then we're adjourned."

The others left the room. Joel caught Caleb's arm.

"Is there something you want to tell me?" Joel pressed, not letting go of his question.

Caleb didn't know whether to laugh or shake his head. The man was acting like Kaye was his sixteen-year-old sister and not a woman who'd been in the army for over a decade and achieved the rank of captain. "We discussed Charlie's sermon. I think both she and I might have left a few burdens down by the river."

Joel cocked his head. "Really?"

"Yup."

"Anything else?"

"What's wrong with you, Joel?"

He frowned as if realizing he was acting like an overprotective brother. "She's been through a lot. I don't want to see her hurt."

"I understand. Your sister's amazing, and I wanted to

tie her ex to one of the bulls in the rodeo and give him a good ride."

"Good thinking."

Caleb patted his friend on the back and walked to the barn. Razor needed a good rubdown.

Later, Caleb stretched out on his bunk, his boots off and sitting beside the bed. His hands were folded behind his head, the events of the day running through his mind. Charlie's preaching had jerked some things in his heart. And Kaye, well, Charlie had gotten to her, too. It still amazed him that when he'd told her that she should listen to Charlie's sermon, those words had echoed in his spirit and he'd nearly winced. *Sometimes there is no explanation for what happens, but heaven knows the reason.*

His heart reverberated with the insight that he'd had no control over Mankiller. Tag being hurt was an accident.

Why was that so hard to accept? Surely he could've done something. Maybe it was from the way he'd grown up. He'd learned early on after his dad died to try to have things just right to ease Mom's burdens, so there was nothing that she or later, one of her boyfriends, could get upset over. If he could have everything in place, things would go smoothly or relatively more smoothly. But if something wasn't right, or things weren't exactly so—he'd lived with too many fallouts to count.

Maybe that was it. Maybe that was why he was so neat. Other cowboys looked at him as weird for how tidy he was.

His thoughts turned to Kaye and the times he'd held her.

He had feelings for her, no matter that this wasn't the right time, no matter that he tried not to, no matter if it scared him stupid. The instant he'd seen Kaye in the driveway, *zap*. He could've run the house for days with all the electricity he'd felt.

His cell rang. Caleb sat up, walked to where he'd left his phone charging and answered.

"Hey, bro."

"Sawyer, how are things going there in Tyler?"

"If I decided to beat my head against the wall, it might be easier."

Caleb laughed. "Going that well, huh?"

"Sometimes what's obvious to outsiders is beyond what insiders can see."

"They can't see their nose on their faces?"

"No, they can't," Sawyer moaned. "I didn't call to report on my trials but to see how you are doing. Are you still at Joel's place?"

Sawyer's concern came through loud and clear. The instant Sawyer had heard about the accident a couple months ago, he'd called. He'd been ready to come to Albuquerque to be with Caleb. Caleb had refused, telling Sawyer he was fine. "It's going well."

"Bro, this is your brother. The guy that suffered through the same thing you did. *It's going well* doesn't cut it."

"Since when did you become my psychologist?"

"Since you took that last punch from Jimmy Morgan."

Jimmy had been the last boyfriend their mother had had before Caleb had petitioned the court to declare him an emancipated minor. If Caleb hadn't stepped in and taken the punch Jimmy threw, it might have killed Sawyer. When Jimmy raised his fist to hit Caleb again, he quietly said, "Try it." Caleb vibrated with determination and conviction. Jimmy backed off. Later, their mother, who stood idly by and watched, defended Jimmy saying Sawyer had provoked him. The boys had left that night for a shelter.

"I ran into Charlie Newman and attended his cowboy church today. He talked about letting go of the mistakes of the past. I've been wrestling with what he said. And when I was talking to Kaye—"

"Kaye who?"

"Captain Brenda Kaye, Joel's sister."

"She's a police officer?"

"No, she's ex-army. Now you want me to tell you the story or do you want to keep interrupting?"

A chuckle came through the phone. "Please continue."

"Kaye is dealing with some heavy stuff from her time in the army and other things. As I was talking to her about those things, I realized what happened with Tag was an accident."

"Thank You, God." The words were barely audible.

"I've been that out of it?" Caleb didn't realize he could be read that easily.

"Yeah, I could've told you that, but you weren't ready to hear it. And I'd like to meet Kaye."

"I think you have a job you're doing."

"True, but I'm almost done. You could capture a picture of her on your phone and send it to me."

"I don't know. Tell you what. How about I trade pictures with you. You send me pictures of the folks giving you a hard time, and I'll send you Kaye's picture."

Sawyer remained silent for several seconds.

"Hey, if we're going to do this, let's be fair."

"Okay. But God's answered my prayers for you. You going to ride pick-up for Kaye?"

"No. I'm having some other pick-up riders do it."

"Why?"

Caleb didn't have a good answer. "Since I've already lined up other riders, they don't need me. And I don't want to cancel on them."

"I think if you've realized it was an accident, then let God finish the healing and ride."

"I'll think about it."

"Don't think. Do." Sawyer hung up.

Caleb pulled the phone away from his ear and stared at it.

Sawyer's words planted a truth in his heart. Could he do it?

"Lord, I need some help here." But he knew that saying God had healed him and acting on it were two different things, and he just didn't know if he could do it. He had the head knowledge, but his heart was a different matter.

Kaye stepped out of Ken Moody's office at city hall. As she walked outside, she found herself smiling. After her talk with Caleb yesterday afternoon, she and God had had a long chat last night. Old pains and disappointments were laid at His feet. Today, the sun seemed to shine brighter and the birds sang sweeter.

Across the street from the city office stood a new coffee/tea/bakery, Sweet Treats. A latte was calling her name and she would answer the call. She hurried across the street and had her hand on the door when she heard, "Whoa, Kaye."

Billye Ludwig Zimmerman waved to her and hurried down the sidewalk, a large gray dog with a wiry coat at her side. She stopped before Sweet Treats. "I'm so glad I saw you because I wanted to talk to you."

Kaye looked at the large dog. "Is he yours?"

Billye looked adoringly down at the dog. "This is Branigan. He's an Irish wolfhound and, aside from my kids, Branigan was one of the few good things I got out of my marriage. Aren't you, big guy?" Billye ruffled the fur on the dog's head. He looked at Billye with loving eyes. "Too bad my ex wasn't as affectionate."

"Want to join me for a latte?" Kaye asked looking down at the dog. "That is if Sweet Treats allows it."

"Oh, you read my mind, but Branigan can't go inside. They have a patio on the side, though."

"Sounds good."

After they ordered their drinks and pastries, they settled at a small table on the porch. Branigan stretched out beside the table. "Br—Kaye, I have a wonderful idea for the rodeo. I have a friend who is a boot maker. He's made a name for himself, and he's willing to donate a custom pair of boots for the winner of a raffle."

"Who is that?"

"Jason Kelly. He's out of San Angelo. My ex, when he wanted to play cowboy and have a really fancy set of boots, contacted Jason. Jason called me last night and asked if he could donate his services to the charity rodeo. I told him I'd get in contact with you."

"He called you? Jason Kelly?" Kaye knew who the man was. His reputation preceded him.

Billye leaned over the table. "Can you believe it? I nearly passed out when he told me who he was. But if he offered to do boots, well, I wasn't going to say no. He heard about the rodeo through some of his connections."

Kaye marveled at how God was spreading the word. "What a fantastic idea. I'd love to add his donation to the rodeo. Give me his number and I'll contact him and get the details."

Billye pulled the boot maker's information out of her purse and handed the paper to Kaye. "You'll like him." She wiggled her eyebrow. "He's not hard on the eyes."

Billye reached down and slipped Branigan part of her muffin. "You're looking better than the last time we met. There's something about you—a glow." Billye rubbed her chin, then her eyes lightened. "Is there something going on between you and that handsome cowboy at your ranch?"

Kaye's hands fumbled with the zipper of her purse. "Why would you ask that?"

"Oh, please. This is Billye Ludwig, your best bud in high school. You could never hide when you had a crush on some boy. You knew when I fell in love with my ex. And why didn't you try to talk me out of it?"

"I did," Kaye replied.

The wind went out of Billye's sails. "Okay, I'll give you that, but you didn't answer my question. Give it up. Why the smile?"

Kaye couldn't keep back her joy. "Lots of things. Yesterday, we went to the cowboy church in the stockyards." Kaye explained about the sermon and how it touched her.

Billye's eyes welled with tears. "Oh, I've prayed for you, friend. Those months after your parents died hurt us all, seeing you pull into yourself and not let anyone in. I just didn't know how to help."

Kaye had been so lost in her own misery that she hadn't realized how others had viewed it.

"I knew why you joined the army, but I lost my best friend. I wanted to talk to you about Tom's proposal, to get your opinion. I knew you weren't crazy about him, but you never said why." She shrugged.

Kaye caught Billye's hand. "I'm sorry. After what happened to my family, I was lost in a fog. I'm surprised I was able to graduate. I should've been there for you. I knew Tom was a selfish jerk at homecoming when his friend gave him his spot on the fifty-yard line but there wasn't enough room for both of you. He let you find your own spot at the side of the bleachers." It had been a pathetic sight to see Billye sitting by herself with that massive mum on her shoulder. Kaye and her date had sat with Billye.

Billye covered Kaye's hand. "My mom told me the same thing. I was just too determined to get married." She took a deep breath. "But enough about me. You still haven't told me about that secret smile. And if I had my guess, I'd say it has something to do with Caleb."

It was like old times. "I could never divert you, could I?"

"Nope." Billye waited.

"Caleb is unique. He's— Well, he's the calm in the midst of the storm." Kaye didn't want to mention the kiss. "And he's got a great horse."

Coffee spurted out of Billye's nose and mouth. They both started laughing. Branigan scrambled from his sprawled position and looked around for the danger. Billye petted her dog, calming him down.

Kaye wiped the tears from her eyes and tried to gain control of her laughter.

"A great horse?" Billye repeated and they both broke out into another fit of laughter.

When Kaye could answer, she said, "Well, Caleb's amazing. He's—"

"That's okay." Billye held up her hand. "Whatever he is, he's caught your eye and put that glow in your cheeks. That's good enough for me."

Kaye grinned back at her friend, feeling as light and joyful as she had before that fatal New Year's Eve. "Yeah, he has."

Billye's eyes softened and her smile reflected the emotion. "It's about time, Brenda Lynn Kaye, that you experience some joy in your life. I want you to know, I missed my best friend while you were gone. There's been no one to take your place." Billye caught Kaye's hand and squeezed. "I'm so glad you're back."

Kaye's heart jerked at her friend's words. She hadn't realized how her pain had affected others, and God was showing her she was not alone.

She'd never been alone.

Her phone rang. Kaye fumbled with her purse and grabbed the phone. "Hello."

"May I speak to Brenda Kaye?"

"This is she." As Kaye listened to the person on the other end, her eyes went wide. "Now?" Kaye eyed her friend. "Okay, then I'll see you in ten minutes at the fairgrounds." When she disconnected the call she turned to Billye. "Would you like to be interviewed by a Myra Taos about the charity rodeo?" Myra was the leading TV reporter in the Dallas/Fort Worth market.

"You're kidding me, aren't you?"

"No. She wants to do a story for tonight's news about the rodeo, and she needs to interview one of the contributors. You can pitch the custom boots. It should bring in more bids."

"That's the girl I knew in high school."

Kaye was beginning to come to terms with that girl she'd left here.

They gathered up their items and started toward the fairgrounds a couple streets away. Branigan trailed behind his master.

"Maybe your dog will be the next TV star."

They looked down at the dog and laughed as they had in high school. It was a good memory.

"So how'd your meeting go in town?" Caleb asked as he and Joel walked into the kitchen. They'd been out most of the day, repairing fences and checking on the cattle. Caleb was suspicious that Joel had checked the fences to avoid having to mess with details of the rodeo.

Before Kaye could answer, Gramps called out from the living room. "Brenda, what are you doing on TV?"

When they'd ridden in this afternoon and put their saddles in the barn, Gramps had been there sitting on a bale of hay. It appeared he was sleeping, but he'd covered himself when he walked out with the guys, saying the barn was finally reorganized.

They all hurried into the living room just as the anchor introduced the piece. Next came Myra on the screen, explaining about the rodeo. Kaye, Billye and Branigan were in the interview piece.

"One of the raffles will be for custom boots by Jason Kelly," Billye explained.

"The outpouring of support has been overwhelming," Kaye added. "Everyone wants to contribute to the funds to buy the seed."

The camera cut back to the reporter. "Jason Kelly is the number-one custom boot maker in the state. This rodeo should be a good one and is sure to touch the hearts of many. Myra Taos, reporting. Back to you in the studio."

All three males looked at Kaye.

"When did that happen?" Gramps asked.

"Yeah, have you been holding out on us, Sis?"

"No. After my meeting with the mayor this morning that no one wanted to go to, I saw Billye. We were talking when the reporter called. She was already here in town and we did the interview."

"I think what Joel meant was when did Jason Kelly donate the boots?" Caleb explained.

"Oh. Billye told me this morning." Caleb's puzzled look joined Joel's and Gramps's. "At least I found out about it this morning when Billye told me."

"How'd you get Jason to donate boots?" Joel asked.

"Yeah, the boots he made for me several years ago set me back a tidy sum," Caleb added. "I was fortunate and caught him before he got famous. Of course, those boots are still my favorite and fit like a glove."

Kaye shrugged. "I'm not certain. He could've heard about it through his rodeo connections, or some of the news reports. That's not important. What matters is he's going to do it."

"It's sure something to see how this is coming together." And it wasn't just the way the rodeo was coming together. Caleb knew there was a way out of the mess his life had turned into.

The next week Tina Linton from the university called. "Kaye, would you like to visit one of the clinics dealing with PTSD?"

"I'd love to. When could we arrange it?"

"Do you have time this afternoon? There is a group session, and I thought it might help you to decide at what level you'd like to work and what certification you'd want."

Kaye wasn't sure, but deep inside she felt this was heaven opening a door. "I'd love to go. Just tell me when and where."

Tina gave her the information, and at one o'clock that afternoon, Kaye sat in a group session of former marines, sailors and soldiers. One of the marines was a woman. The guy leading the session, Ben Sisk, introduced Kaye.

"This is ex-captain Brenda Kaye. She's going to be sitting in on our session today. She's training to work with vets with PTSD."

Kaye wanted to object and say she was thinking about it, but one guy asked, "Where'd you serve?"

"I was part of the all-female Team Lioness in Baghdad."

He folded his arms over his chest, but Kaye saw the respect in his eyes. "I heard about them. If we had to pat down a woman, we needed a female soldier or else…" The man shook his head.

"True," Kaye answered. "We had some tricky situations."

The session started and Kaye listened to the vets recount stories they didn't know how to handle. Finally, one man turned to Kaye. "What about you, Captain? You got any baggage?"

Ben held up his hand. "She's just here as an observer."

"That's okay, Ben. I don't mind answering since everyone here has been so up-front and honest." She turned to the man who asked the question. "When I was in Baghdad, I was assigned as liaison with the women of a certain neighborhood. I got to know them, like them, laugh with them and discovered what their fears and dreams were and what they wanted for their children. The army rebuilt one of their schools, and their girls were going to attend.

"We met at a café to celebrate the school's opening and I brought gifts for them, books for the girls. When I leaned over to get the gifts—" she took a deep breath "—the suicide bomber walked in and detonated himself. I was the only survivor. The school never opened and all the work I'd done—poof. Gone."

"Wow, you have any nightmares?" the man asked.

"Yeah, and guilt," Kaye added.

Everyone in the group shook their heads in understanding. After ninety minutes the session ended. Every member of the group stopped to shake her hand. When the lone female paused in front of Kaye, her eyes said it all. "It's good to talk to another female vet. There were things that happened that men don't understand, and I don't want to share in group. I hope you come back."

Kaye understood only too well. "Thanks," she whispered and knew in that instant, this was the path God wanted her to travel.

Once they were alone in the large room and putting up

chairs, Ben said, "Once you start your training, I'd love for you to come here and help. And you definitely can do your training hours here."

"Thanks, but—"

"What?"

"I might need more counseling myself before I can help anyone." She couldn't meet Ben's gaze.

"Kaye, we all have nightmares."

She stopped and understood Ben's message that he, too, had his share of nightmares.

"It doesn't disqualify you. In fact, it gives you street cred and, as you go through the classes and certification, you'll find a way to deal with it."

On her drive home, there was a peace in her soul. She'd found her way. She wasn't to the end, but she'd started on the right path. And she wanted to share her discovery with Caleb.

When Kaye drove up to the house, the driveway was filled with satellite trucks from the national network. Kaye managed to squeeze her jeep around several trucks and parked next to Caleb's trailer. She slipped inside the barn, wondering what was going on.

Caleb stood in the shadows, watching the house.

"What's going on?"

"Seems Myra's piece caught the attention of her network executives in New York and they sent one of their reporters out to the ranch to interview you."

Kaye glanced at the house. "Haven't they heard about calling for an interview?"

"Apparently, they did. Gramps took the call. When they showed up, he fessed up and said they'd called yesterday."

Kaye pursed her lips and shook her head.

"It will be good publicity for the rodeo. Myra's interview seems to have exploded this thing. Seems another couple radio stations called today from El Paso, San Angelo and San Antonio. It's as if the western part of this state wants to help. With national exposure, who knows, you might get cowboys from all over the nation to come. And the more money we generate, the more it will help the ranchers."

He had a point. The rodeo was for the ranchers. "What about the other board members?"

"They've talked with the other members at the fair-grounds. Nan followed them here. They want to interview you and put the piece on tonight."

"Okay."

As she started out of the barn, Caleb called out to her. "How did the counseling group go?"

"I'll tell you tonight."

After the news piece ran on the TV, the house phone immediately started to ring. It had been a wonderful advertisement. Finally around ten, Kaye found time to talk. They walked out to the corral.

"So tell me how the counseling session went," Caleb said.

"I felt at home. They understood in a unique way. When I talked about my flashbacks, no one was shocked or looked at me as if I was crazy." She looked out into the night. "It was a burden lifted off my shoulders."

"Good. You're on the right road." He hesitated, opened his mouth then closed it. "You're a strong woman, Kaye. Don't sell yourself short. I don't."

Her eyes watered. "It helps to have someone believe in you."

"I do and am awed by your courage."

Throwing her arms around him, she hugged him. When she stepped back, she touched his cheek. "Thank you."

They stared into each other's eyes. He started to lower his head when the back door slammed.

"Brenda, you've got a phone call."

She sighed. "Thanks, Gramps." Stepping away, she said, "I think this publicity might be bigger than we think."

Rodeo or no, spring was branding time, and all the area ranchers helped each other. Caleb and Joel helped at the neighbors' ranches, while Kaye stayed at the house, continuing to work on the rodeo. After a week of branding, the final day the ranchers were at the Double "K" Ranch.

"I'll say, things sure have taken off. I feel like we're in the middle of a stampede with all the folks showing up in town," John Burkett, the closest neighbor, said.

"Things have heated up since the network spot," Caleb replied.

"Well, my son and daughter are going to compete. Carrie's going to do the barrel racing and Jon is doing the calf scramble." He nodded toward some of the calves they'd just branded. "I heard that Joel is going to use these calves in the scramble."

The men heard an engine and looked up and saw the jeep.

"Lunch is here, guys," Joel announced.

"I never thought I'd see that girl again," John muttered.

Caleb's heart raced at the sight of Kaye. In spite of the work on the rodeo, Kaye had taken time out of her activities and brought them lunch. Diane Burkett was in the jeep with Kaye. The day before, the men had been at the Burkett spread, and Diane had worked with another wife providing lunch.

Kaye brought her jeep to a stop. "Hey, guys, anyone hungry?"

"Yes," echoed through the air.

"Diane and I have barbecue, beans, potato salad and cookies. And gallons of tea. Come and get it."

The men finished up their work. Caleb walked to the vehicle.

"Caleb, can you get the card table out of the back?" Kaye called out. She didn't look at him again as the two women worked in tandem to get the food out of the jeep.

"Thanks for thinking of us," Caleb said as he set up the table.

"Part of the job." Kaye continued putting out the food. "I remember my mom doing this when we were growing up. And cowboys don't change. They're still hungry during branding time." She paused, a smile lighting her face. "As if I could've forgotten."

The men gathered around. After a quick prayer, the guys dug in.

"Are you going to join us, Sis?" Joel grabbed a paper plate.

"Of course. I loved this new place in town. When we had it the other night, it was to die for."

Riley's Bar-B-Q was on the sacks the food came in. "It's been there eight years, Sis."

Kaye ignored the comment. "I served Gramps a plate before I came. Beware, he told me this was the last day he's staying close to the house. He's done with all the babying."

Over the next thirty minutes, Caleb watched as Kaye greeted each man, asked about their families and caught up on her time away. She made sure all the men put their plates and cups in a trash sack. Diane also talked to each rancher. Once everything was back in her jeep, the women drove off.

John walked to Caleb and Joel's sides. "That sister of yours, Joel, is a mighty sharp woman. I think some single man needs to snap her up."

"I'm telling you, I'm praying that guy's going to get on the stick. He's late." Joel slapped John on the back and they went to finish the last of the branding.

That man would be a blessed man. If only things were different....

That afternoon Kaye contacted Jason Kelly.

"Do you need something else from me, Miss Kaye?" Jason asked.

She had to smile. Jason addressing her as Miss Kaye told her he was a true Texas boy. "I want to order a pair of boots."

"For yourself? I can measure you when I come to the rodeo."

"They're not for me. They are for Caleb Jensen."

The boot maker remained quiet.

"You did a pair of boots for him a while back." Her heart beat faster and she began to feel like this idea was a mistake.

"I remember Caleb. He was one of my first customers. Those boots I made him have been some of the best advertisement I've had."

"Can you make a new pair of boots for him? Do you still have his measurements?"

"Of course I do. I never throw away a customer's measurements in case they want to order new boots."

"Well, I'd like to order another pair for him." She wanted to thank Caleb for his help.

They spent the next few minutes discussing details of what leather she wanted and the particular style. Jason directed her to his website and she picked the leather and color.

"Anything special you want on them?"

Kaye thought a moment. Did she want to fancy up the

boots? "Can you put an outline of the state of Texas on the side?"

"I can do that."

They discussed price and when he could have them done.

"I can bring the finished boots to the rodeo with me. Will that do?" Jason asked.

"That's perfect. Thank you." She hung up.

"What's perfect?" Caleb asked.

Kaye's gaze went to the entrance to the dining room. Caleb stood there, dusty with his hair wild. How long had the man been standing there?

"The arrangements I just made. You finished for the day?" Hopefully he would not probe further into the conversation he just overheard.

He looked down at himself. "We are." He stood there, his hat in his hands.

Her heart started beating hard. The man looked entirely too good standing there, covered with dirt. She'd been noticing too much about him and wanted to be held in his arms again. Caleb wormed his way into her heart. And now that God had started healing the wounds left by her parents' deaths, she found a deep joy. The man standing before her now was part of that joy.

"Would you like to go out to dinner tonight?"

Well, if he'd asked her if she wanted to stand on her head and sing the army anthem, the Caisson Song, she couldn't have been more surprised. She studied him.

His mouth curved in a shy smile. "I feel like I'm sixteen asking my first girl out."

"That's okay. I feel the same way, except the girl thing." They laughed.

"Fort Worth?"

"Yeah. I thought we could have our pick of any place we want."

"I'd like that."

He nodded. "Let's plan on leaving around five." He walked out of the house.

A date.

He'd asked her for a date. Her heart fluttered. That teenage Brenda was still there deep inside. A tear slipped down her cheek.

Chapter Eleven

"Oh, my, that is one of the best burgers I've ever had." Kaye took a drink of her Dr. Pepper.

Caleb took the last cowboy fry that came with his burger and popped it into his mouth. "I found this place several years ago. The guy who runs it is an ex-rodeo man. Whenever I come through Fort Worth, I have one of his burgers."

They'd tried to go to several fancy restaurants, but on Friday night the wait was anywhere from a half hour to an hour and a half. He suggested the Crooked Boot instead.

"Well, I'll say, there's nothing better than a burger with fries." She shook her head. "My ex used to complain I had plain tastes, along with being boring and monotonous."

"There's nothing wrong with being plain about a good burger, as any cowboy can tell you. As for monotonous, if being dependable is monotonous I'll take boring every time. In my humble opinion, there's something seriously wrong with your ex."

Her eyes warmed and she smiled. "Of course, when you're overseas at a posting, sometimes it's just easier not to ask what they're serving you." She grinned. "Didn't the Apostle Paul say something about 'just eat what's put in front of you and not ask where it came from'? I had a wonderful dish with chunks of meat floating in gravy while I was visiting a village in northern Iraq. You ate it with flatbread. It was delicious until I asked what it was."

He waited for her to tell him what she ate. "And?"

"Well, let's just say I'm glad to have a hamburger with meat I can identify."

"I'm glad I could grant your wish."

She settled back into the wooden chair out on the restaurant porch. "So have you decided what you're going to do? Are you going to go back and work the rodeo or do something else?"

Caleb ran his fingers over the outside of his paper cup. "I haven't decided yet." Since Charlie had preached about giving things to God, his heart felt lighter, but he still had no direction on what to do. Something was there, making things hazy, and he couldn't figure out what. "You still on board with getting your counseling certificate?"

"Yes, I am. Of course, with all the rodeo stuff, I haven't had time to look over class schedules, but I have applied. Now I have to decide how—as a social worker, counselor, psychologist or psychiatrist. How long do I want to go to school? I'm letting that decision stew while I take care of the rodeo."

They finished their meal and walked to the truck. A large park was across from the little hamburger stand. "C'mon." He took her hand as she stepped down into the street. He didn't release it as they crossed the street. Kaye didn't object.

"Watching you deal with this rodeo, well—I've been impressed."

She shrugged. "Being organized helped. I guess I just had an untapped talent inside me and the army found it.

Looking at your trailer, you understand the importance of order."

His brow arched.

"Remember, we used the microwave in your trailer after that lightning strike."

Okay, that made sense. "Living in that small an area, it's important to be organized." He stopped on a small bridge that spanned the creek running through the park.

"You don't mind so small an area?" She looked into his face.

The woman was just the right size, tall enough where he could easily see her incredible blue eyes and her lips—

"No, it doesn't bother me. It's mine. The house I grew up in was rented. We had nothing that belonged to us except our horses, truck and horse trailer. That trailer sitting at the ranch is mine."

She thought about his words. "I can understand that. I've moved from one base to another, and all I took was my duffel bag."

Again, they had something in common.

"Do you know this is my first official date?"

Kaye turned toward him. "I find that hard to believe that you've reached the ripe old age of—" She waited.

"Thirty-two."

"The ripe old age of thirty-two and not officially asked a girl on a date."

The realization knocked him off center. "Well, I didn't date in high school because I worked to help support Sawyer and myself. When I was working the rodeo, there were lots of gatherings and parties. I'd go to a party, but the woman I was hanging out with knew about the party and it was just understood we'd go together. But to actually ask someone on a date, you're the first."

"Whoa, you're in worse shape than me."

"I don't know. I think I'm just at the right age to be asking a girl out." He pulled her gently into his arms, allowing her the chance to back away. She didn't. As he bent down, she went up until their lips met. Kaye wrapped her arms around him and eagerly kissed him back. When he pulled back, he smiled.

"That wasn't your first kiss," she said.

"You're right, but I think it was the best."

"I can't believe it's almost here," Gramps said over dinner. "Y'all have been running around like chickens with your heads cut off today. I'm tired just watching y'all."

Last-minute details had filled every waking hour for Kaye and the members of her committee.

"Imagine if I'd been trying to do this thing." Joel popped the last of his steak in his mouth. "Each rodeo event is maxed out and all the booths are assigned to different groups. And I've got enough calves for the scramble for the kids."

"You still owe me, brother." Kaye's words were softened by her smile.

"What can I say?" He shrugged.

Yesterday, the fairgrounds manager had given her the checklist of what needed to be done. She also had a checklist of accommodations for the riders. Different ranchers and people in town had volunteered a bedroom in their house for cowboys and cowgirls if they didn't bring their own trailers. Since everyone had volunteered their prize money to the ranch fund, the ranchers were eager to help.

Seeing all her old high school friends had brought Kaye countless memories, yet her reminiscences were not bittersweet, but warm celebrations of her youth. God was healing her one memory at a time.

She couldn't believe the biggest change that occurred

over the past six weeks was her growing relationship with Caleb. His first date. She'd been his first date. After that night they'd talked and spent time with each other. He helped after dinner when she worked on the rodeo issues. Joel grumbled that Caleb was building up too many good-guy points that no one could compare with him. Caleb only laughed at him.

As Kaye cleaned up the kitchen, Caleb joined her. "It's not your turn. Go sit down with Gramps and Joel. You grilled." Joel, Caleb and Kaye had made a pact—the person who made dinner didn't clean up. Their rotating calendar was stuck on the refrigerator.

"They're not the person I want to spend time with."

Kaye stared at him, then looked down at the dishes in the sink, suddenly shy and feeling that teenage thing again where you acted stupid. "Okay, be prepared to load the dishwasher."

They finished the dishes in record time while Kaye tried to tamp down the teen reaction. What was wrong with her? She'd led men, ordered them in stressful situations, composed strategy, gone through countless scenarios where she had no problem dealing with things. But with Caleb, her mind turned to mush.

When Caleb put away the last pot, he turned to her.

"Want to go stargazing?"

His suggestion captured her imagination. "I like that idea."

He held out his hand. She slid her hand in his and they walked outside. Caleb had placed a couple folding chairs in the yard. "I didn't think we had any of those chairs."

"You didn't. I have them in my trailer."

He guided her to a chair, then sat beside her. The clear night made the stars dance in the sky.

"Sometimes, when I was overseas, I'd look at the night sky and think of home. There was a comfort in that."

"Sawyer and I loved stargazing. It was our favorite pastime. Our dad used to take us out and show us the stars."

There was something—a tone in his voice—that caught Kaye's attention. "Tell me about your brother."

"Sawyer's three years younger than me. We were and are best buds, especially after Dad's death. We were two scared kids who learned to rely on each other. Sometimes we sneaked out of the house and sat in the field behind the house and watched the stars." He fell silent, as if lost in a memory.

Kaye understood about sharing those special moments. She'd had that with her dad.

He came back to her from the past memories and gave a short laugh. "We got really good at spotting the different constellations. I toyed with the idea of becoming an astronomer when I was in high school." He slipped his arm around her shoulders.

"Why didn't you?"

"Life got in the way."

"But your brother got his masters."

"He did."

Kaye knew how life got in the way. She rested her head on his shoulder and they quietly shared their disappointments. But her feelings for this man who'd sacrificed his future for his brother only grew. How different was Caleb's view than her ex. If he wanted it, he went for it, no matter the consequences or the cost.

Razor trotted up to the edge of the fence and greeted them.

"I think my horse is jealous," Caleb whispered.

"Or he just wants a treat."

"You're pretty good at reading horses," he teased.

"No. I'm good at reading males, human and equine."

He arched his brow.

"You remember I spent a lot of years around mostly males in uniform before I went to Iraq and my commander established the all-female battalion to deal with the local women. You learn quickly to read body language."

They laughed and walked inside to get Razor a treat. After they fed Razor a carrot, Caleb walked Kaye to the back door and kissed her good-night.

The next morning at breakfast, Kaye and Caleb kept exchanging looks. When she walked to the coffeemaker for another cup, Caleb joined her.

"I would've brought the coffeepot to you."

He stepped close enough that his body brushed hers and he held out his mug. "I know."

Kaye bit back her smile, but high school giddiness bubbled up. She poured him a cup of coffee.

"Thank you."

Her heart nearly melted at his tone.

"Anyone else want coffee?" Kaye turned to the table and held up the pot.

Joel rolled his eyes. As Kaye sat down, the phone rang. Joel answered it.

"Yeah, he's here." Joel held out the phone. "It's for you."

Caleb stood and took the phone receiver. "Yes." Caleb looked at the people seated at the table. When his gaze locked with hers, Kaye's heart skipped a beat. "I'm working a charity rodeo a week from this Saturday near Fort Worth."

Kaye's muscles tightened and her stomach rebelled the longer Caleb was on the phone. "I understand. There's time, but a lot of work still needs to be done." He looked at the people sitting at the table. "I'll think about it." He hung up and walked to the table.

When he didn't say anything, Kaye leaned over her plate. "Well, are you going to tell us what that was about?"

"Sis."

She ignored the warning in her brother's voice. "It sounded like whatever that call was it would affect our event."

Gramps's steady stare added to her brother's objection.

"That was the head of the Western Rodeo Association. There's a rodeo in Oklahoma City tomorrow and their pick-up rider got sick. I'm the closest guy to fill in. I've filled in for him before."

"I don't see a problem." Gramps grabbed his mug and downed the last of his coffee.

"You should consider it," Joel added. "We've got things under control here, so why not?"

Kaye could hardly believe her ears. Why were her brother and grandfather urging Caleb to do this? "There are tons of last-minute details that come up."

"I agree. Things are getting hectic around here. I don't think I should leave."

The knot in Kaye's stomach eased and suddenly her eyes felt wet. Echoes of Richard shivered through her. When the phone rang, and they had some gig, it didn't matter what the two of them had planned, he was out the door without discussing it with her.

"I think our stockman might arrive this weekend and I want to be here to help him with the animals and get them settled in," Caleb explained.

That call at breakfast haunted Kaye all day long. Her trip into town to talk to the fairgrounds manager about some last-minute decisions was spent telling herself Caleb wasn't Richard, but the tension didn't leave. She'd seen this pattern before. The first time there was a good reason, but it was the countless times afterward excuses weren't needed.

Kaye's morning meeting with Ken worked out the last-minute kinks of the rodeo.

Twenty minutes later, Kaye left the county building. Walking to her car, she heard her name called. Kaye turned and saw Billye with Branigan.

"I'm glad I ran into you while I was in town. I have about a half hour before I have to pick up Amanda. I wanted to look at the booth you've assigned the church. The ladies' auxiliary wanted to see how we're going to split the space. They want cell phone pics of it to plan their part, as if they haven't lived here forever and seen the booths countless times before."

As they walked to the fairgrounds, Billye glanced at Kaye. "What's wrong?"

"What are you talking about?"

"Oh, friend, don't try to fake me out."

Kaye fought off the fears that had been dogging her heels since that call this morning. They stopped before the booth assigned to their church.

Billye grasped her shoulders. "Why aren't you smiling and giddy? This rodeo has taken off. I've never seen so much excitement from the townsfolk. There's not a person who isn't thinking of some way to add to this rodeo. I'm getting calls from folks I don't know, after our segment aired on the network, asking me if they can help. Or send money. And here you are, looking like you lost your best friend."

Kaye's knees went weak and she leaned against the booth.

"Sweetie, what is it?"

Kaye told her about the call Caleb got this morning.

"He told the man he'd think about it. He didn't say he'd do it. So what's the problem?"

"He might."

"Is he planning on deserting you? Not coming back?"

Hearing Billye put her fears into words, it sounded petty and small. "No, he isn't going to desert us."

"Then why borrow trouble?"

"You're right."

That night at dinner, the phone rang again.

Kaye answered this time. "May I speak to Caleb Jensen? This is Steve Carter." The big boss that called earlier.

Kaye held out the phone. "It's for you, Caleb."

Kaye sat down and watched Caleb, her fear roaring back.

"I'm sorry, Steve. I thought about it, but I'm not interested. It's cutting things mighty close." Caleb fell silent, listening. "Twice the rate? Really?"

Her stomach bottomed out.

Joel's brow arched. "Wow," he whispered.

Caleb placed the receiver on his chest and turned toward the table. "What do you think?"

"I'd say you can't afford not to. If you want to start a breeding ranch, that money will come in handy," Joel replied. "You could've bought that little filly you saw the other day in Fort Worth."

"I'd say if you can guarantee to be back in time to help with our shindig, go for it," Gramps added.

Caleb turned to Kaye. "What do you think?"

Her heart felt torn in two. Caleb's words echoed her ex-husband's explanation that he wanted to play with his group one more time to get money for the new couch they wanted. The one time turned into two, then ten. "If you want to go, that's fine." The words sounded hollow.

Caleb put the phone back up to his ear. "Steve, I can't.

I'm obligated here." He hung up the phone and returned to the dinner table.

They finished the meal in silence. Joel cleaned up the dishes while Kaye walked into the formal dining room and looked over the spreadsheet on the table. She saw nothing, fear blinding her eyes.

"If you don't let him go, he'll always wonder."

She jerked, looking up at her grandfather, who stood on the other side of the table. "What do you mean? I told Caleb he could go. It was his choice."

Gramps sat down in the chair at the end of the table. "No, that's not what you did. You said the words, but your voice said 'don't go.' You made it an impossible situation for him, because he would be wrong any way he chose."

Words of defense popped into her head, wanting to deny it, but she closed her lips around the excuse.

"If you don't encourage that man to go and face his fears, he will always wonder about it. He won't be whole. And neither will you. You'll always wonder, and not trust Caleb. Is this about Caleb or about your ex?"

Kaye struggled with the truth. Gramps was right, but the echoes of another similar situation wrapped steel talons around her heart. Hadn't she given this to God? So why was she struggling with this now? "I'm afraid, Gramps. What if one time leads to another? What if he discovers he can't give up traveling and the freedom it gives?"

"And what if he discovers he doesn't want to travel anymore? If he goes, you both will know the answer to the question. It will be settled and that fear will lose its power. You'll know that that young man is nothing like your ex. And you'll know he wants to be here."

He'd hit the nail square on the head.

"Your grandmother was afraid when I went off to college, then when my number came up in the draft. But when I was in Korea, I wrote the woman every day. Our love endured, and there was nothing that could shake us.

"Once I came home, we married and I finished my degree." He leaned forward and took Kaye's hand. "I know that man loves you. Anyone with eyes could see. Trust him."

"You're right, Gramps."

"He's out there in his trailer." He stood and kissed her cheek. "This time, it is your choice with your loved one."

Gramps's parting comment nearly knocked her off her chair.

As she sat there, praying, the scripture passage "perfect love casts out all fear" came to her mind.

"Okay, Lord." She needed to talk to Caleb.

Caleb sat in the barn on a bale of hay. He hadn't planned on working the rodeo in Oklahoma City, but Steve sounded desperate. He could make it. And double the money. That would help with buying some land and breeding stock. When he'd looked into Kaye's eyes, he'd known he couldn't leave her. Her mouth may have said it was fine to go, but her eyes said "don't listen to my words."

He understood about her ex-husband and her fears. Professional cowboys traveled the circuit. It'd taken him a while to understand he judged all women using his mother as the standard. A woman had to prove she wasn't like his mom. But could he live in the shadow of Kaye's first husband, always fearing he'd do the wrong thing?

But as Steve kept calling, it was as if God was saying that Caleb needed to get back up on that horse, face his fears and walk in faith.

"Caleb."

His head jerked up at Kaye's voice. She slowly walked into the barn and sat next to him. She grabbed his hand.

"I want you to go and work for your friend." Her hand squeezed his, but she didn't look at him. "You have to face your doubts and fears. If you don't, you'll be running like I was running."

His hand cupped her chin and raised it. "Are you serious?"

An uncomfortable laugh rang in her throat. "I am, and I know what I'm talking about. Remember the Reverend Charlie's words."

The words burned in his brain.

"You'll have to hurry back, but I think you should work this weekend. Between Joel and the others on the rodeo board, we should be able to handle things here."

He knew it had cost her to come out to him, encouraging him to go. "Steve has been a good friend and always more than generous with me. I've spent a couple Thanksgivings and Christmases with him and his family. Letting him down is hard. Besides, the money is great."

"Then please call him now and tell him you can work." She brushed a kiss across his lips.

He pulled her to his chest and hugged her. "You're a gem," he whispered into her ear.

She shook her head. "No. I'm just a practical woman, and this makes sense." They kissed and she left the barn.

In his trailer, Caleb took his cell phone from where he'd left it on the dresser and called Steve, telling him he'd take the job.

"I'm glad you changed your mind. I was afraid I'd have to cancel the bareback riding if I didn't have a pick-up rider. Thanks, friend. Can you be in Oklahoma City by three o'clock tomorrow afternoon?"

"I'll be there." Caleb ended the call.

He knew that Kaye had fought her way through her fear, and that encouraged him. Besides, if she saw he was nothing like her ex-husband, he might not have to live in that small man's shadow. As he started to pack his trailer, getting it ready for the long drive tomorrow, his phone rang. When he looked at the caller ID, he smiled.

"Hey, Sawyer, what's up?"

"I wanted to talk to you, see how things are going on that charity rodeo."

"Everything is in place. You thinking of coming?"

"I am."

Caleb nearly dropped the phone. "To compete? Are you finished with the job?"

"It's winding down. I'm next scheduled to go to Tucumcari, so on the way there, I thought I'd stop and see you. I might try to compete. I'm not that old that I can't ride and rope."

"I don't know, Sawyer. You might just want to enter the calf scramble. You know, if you haven't been riding, you might be rusty."

"Can't be. I'm younger than you, Caleb."

Now was the time to hint at what he was thinking. Sawyer and Caleb always talked to each other before they had major life changes. "I've been sorting out what happened in Albuquerque. I've wanted to quit for some time, only the accident made me face it. I want to settle down and buy a place and breed stock for the rodeo. With the accident, well, I didn't know what to do. I'm going to quit, but I'm doing one last rodeo in OKC, which they're paying me a handsome fee for. I need to ride once more. Put those bad memories to rest."

The line remained silent, worrying Caleb.

"About time. I was wondering how long it would take you," Sawyer replied, a lightness in his voice. "Caleb, you're the best at what you do, but I understand wanting a home. The last real home we had was that apartment behind the church in Plainview."

"So you like that idea?"

"I do, and although I haven't seen Joel's sister since you never sent me that picture, I've heard something in your voice when you've talked about her."

His brother's comment came as a shock to Caleb. He didn't realize he'd been that obvious.

"Cat got your tongue?"

"Sawyer, in spite of what's happened to her, Kaye hasn't ever let that tragedy stop her. She's directing this entire charity rodeo. She's truly amazing—"

"Unlike Mom." Sawyer filled in the balance of Caleb's sentence.

"There's no comparison."

"You're that serious?"

Caleb surprised himself with his declaration. "I am, I think."

"What's that supposed to mean?"

"Well, I don't know." Caleb felt stupider by the moment, but there'd been something nagging at him. "I guess if you always wanted something, then when you get it, you don't know how to handle it." Caleb rubbed his neck. "I guess I'm unsure of how to act. You knew what to expect with Mom, but were always hoping for better. With Kaye, she gives her best no matter what she feels. I guess her time in the army taught her that."

"Or she's one remarkable lady." Sawyer nailed it.

"You can meet her yourself when you come to the rodeo."

"That's fine."

"Then I'll see you the end of next week." Sawyer hung up.

Caleb sat for a moment, mulling over his feelings. He

kinda, sorta thought he was in love? How'd that work? He'd always wanted a strong, independent woman, the opposite of his mom, who couldn't stand on her own and be a helpmate, so when he found a woman who could contribute and pull her own weight, he wasn't exactly sure how to act. He knew what to expect from a woman like his mom, but with Kaye he didn't.

As Caleb packed up his trailer, getting it ready to travel, he recalled his talk with Kaye yesterday. That had been the first time he'd ever shared with a woman what had happened to Sawyer and himself. But as he'd talked about it, the memories had no pain with them. When he'd prayed the other day down by the river, God had started a healing. As he'd tackled each ugly memory, he'd discovered it hurt less to relive the incident. He felt such a freedom that he couldn't put it into words, but he knew a new path was opening for him.

"Lord, as I go to the rodeo, be with me." The verse in Mark came to mind, for with God all things are possible. This was possible.

At six o'clock the next morning, Caleb loaded Razor in his trailer. Kaye, Joel and Gramps stood watching him.

"You want another cup of coffee?" Gramps's words broke into the silence. Breakfast had been a tense affair, everyone on edge, not knowing what to say. "You got one of the travel mugs for coffee?"

The sky was cloudless and the temperature was already in the seventies, so why did it feel so cold? Kaye wondered.

"I'm good. I'd like to get on the road. I want to be in Oklahoma City by midafternoon to get Razor settled. He likes to have a few hours to settle in before we work."

Gramps laughed. "He sounds like a spoiled horse."

"I'm afraid so, but then again lots of cowboys depend on Razor being on top of his game."

Kaye wanted her brother and Gramps to leave so she could talk to Caleb privately. Joel seemed to understand.

"There's something I need to show you in the barn, Gramps." Joel pulled at his sleeve.

"What?"

Joel nodded toward his sister and Caleb.

"Huh, yeah, I wanted to see that thing."

Gramps walked with Joel into the barn.

Once alone Kaye stood there, searching for the words, praying Caleb would make the first move.

"I talked to my brother last night," Caleb began. "I think he's going to sign up to compete at the charity rodeo. You can meet him."

She welcomed his words. "I'd like that. I'll check with Mike later to see if he registers." She knew he needed to face the past, but it frightened her, nonetheless. She stepped closer. "Be careful, Caleb."

Her words seemed to startle him.

"I don't think I've ever had someone say that to me."

His comment awed her. "Surely your brother told you to be careful."

Caleb cupped her chin. "Kaye, you're talking about guys. I knew he wanted me to come back safely, wished me God's speed and protection, but guys don't say 'be careful.' Did any man in the army tell another to be careful?"

"Sure they did. Well, they'd wish them luck. Or say 'Watch your back,' but— Okay, it's a girl thing."

He smiled down into her eyes. "Thank you. Your words mean more than you know."

"You have my prayers, too."

He brushed his lips across hers. "But I will say, this is

a new experience for me, coming home to a ranch full of people. One in particular."

His words wrapped around her heart. She nodded and stepped back, then watched Caleb drive down their driveway.

His comforting words reassured her, but the voice of doubt whispered in her ear: *you've seen this before.*

"But this is a different man. A good one."

Caleb pulled into a gas station in Ardmore. After gassing his truck, he bought a large coffee. He checked Razor to make sure the horse was doing fine. "Last leg of the trip, Razor."

He climbed into the truck and headed out. Kaye's warning, asking him to be careful, found its way straight into his heart. Her words had taken his breath away.

In her smile, he could see a future. A woman who a man could depend on.

But was he the right man?

Did he want to be the right man?

Yes, he wanted to try.

So how was he going to do that? He didn't know, but he was going to come up with a way.

After settling Razor into the temporary stall, Caleb checked in with the business office. The afternoon quickly passed, with several old friends welcoming him with open arms.

Once the rodeo began, Caleb saddled Razor and walked him to a waiting area by the arena. He paused and checked the cinch on his saddle before he mounted Razor. "Okay, Razor, you ready, boy?" Caleb patted his horse's shoulder.

Razor nodded and they rode into the arena. The announcer came on the PA system.

"Okay, folks, next up is the saddle-bronc riding. And welcome back Caleb Jensen as one of our pick-up riders tonight."

The announcer's words caught Caleb by surprise, since the pick-up riders weren't normally acknowledged.

The audience began clapping, as did the cowboys gathered around the pens at the end of the arena. Caleb felt their welcome and support. No one threw an accusing look at him. Only understanding and admiration did he find in those eyes. He rode out into the arena and lifted his hat, acknowledging their applause.

Riding back to his spot, he settled himself on Razor, focusing on his job. The paralyzing fear he expected didn't appear, but a peace and assurance from above filled his heart.

"Thank You, Father," he whispered before the metal gate opened and the first horse and cowboy jumped into the ring. It was the last time he had to think for the next hour.

Chapter Twelve

The day passed quickly, filled with endless last-minute details for the rodeo, leaving Kaye no time to stew over Caleb's absence. A week before the scheduled rodeo, it seemed everyone came out of the woodwork. Two radio stations wanted interviews. Last-minute registrations poured in.

Kaye moved her files and Joel's computer to the small office on the fairgrounds formerly used by Ken. He helped her access the internet so she would be up and running. During the day, there was a continuous stream of people who stopped by, asking questions.

That night after dinner, Joel finished going over his arrangements for the coming weekend. As Kaye walked into the dining room, she heard her brother whistling. She stopped. She hadn't heard her brother whistle in a number of years, but as she recalled, while he was growing up, the man always whistled.

"Hey, Sis." He frowned. "Anything wrong? Something happen with the rodeo?"

"No."

"Then what?" He appeared truly puzzled.

"You were whistling."

He sat back in his chair. "I was, wasn't I?"

"That's the first time I've heard you whistling since we were kids."

He crossed his arms over his chest. He remained quiet for several moments, then finally said, "I guess you're right." He went back to finalizing the plans for the rodeo.

Kaye sat at the table and buried herself in the schedule, making sure she knew what needed to be taken care of each day before the rodeo.

Kaye didn't know when Joel left, but Gramps stuck his head in to say good-night.

"Don't stay up too late because I think you'll probably get some early-morning calls and you'll need a clear head."

"Thanks, Gramps." He turned away, but Kaye called out, "Gramps."

He stopped.

"I have a question for you. When was the last time you heard Joel whistle?"

"Today."

"No, I mean in the time I was gone, did he whistle like he used to do when he was growing up?"

Gramps walked into the room and sat down. She could see him thinking about the question. "Now that you asked about it, no, I can't remember him whistling. But he has been the past couple days."

Kaye stood. "That's what I remember, too."

"Why do you ask?"

"I think that maybe this rodeo is something that Joel needed. Maybe he lost part of himself when he had to come back and take over the ranch."

"You might be onto something there."

"Of course, maybe I've been thinking too much and it's time to go to bed."

Gramps went to his room. Kaye walked into the kitchen

to get a drink of tea and saw Joel sitting outside on the picnic table. She grabbed another glass, filled it with tea and took it out to her brother.

"Thanks, Sis."

"What are you doing out here?"

"I thought I'd check on the horses in the barn and just wanted to enjoy the evening. All that paperwork is a royal pain."

"Hey, welcome to my world."

He shook his head.

"I have a question for you."

"Okay."

"Do you ever miss the rodeo circuit? You gave up on your dream and came back here to take care of the place. Did you ever resent having to come home?"

He rubbed the back of his neck; his brows dipped. "Well, I haven't thought about it that way."

"You had to stop chasing your dream to take care of me and this ranch, then I turned around and left the instant I could."

Joel wrapped his arm around her shoulders. "No, I didn't resent it. You're my sister and I couldn't just leave you to try to run this place yourself."

"But I left you."

"Sis, I'm proud of all you accomplished in the army. And no, I never resented it."

"But you're whistling."

His brow furrowed. "What are you talking about?"

"You were whistling in the dining room. You did it when we were growing up but quit after Mom and Dad died." She waited on his answer.

"You're right, but I don't have any answers for you. But know this, I never held it against you that you left. I was proud when anyone asked me about my sister, the captain."

Later, when she was in her room, she wished she could give her brother his dream back.

The rodeo final would be held tomorrow afternoon. As Caleb and Razor had worked tonight, there had not been a single instance where Caleb didn't feel in control. He had only received thumbs-up from the cowboys at the coliseum, or "glad to see you back." What happened before wasn't an issue.

As Caleb took care of Razor after the rodeo, a certainty sprang to life in him that his time as a professional pick-up rider was over, and he looked forward to the next stage of his life as a married man and rancher. And the only woman he wanted as his wife was Kaye. No, Captain Brenda Kaye.

He walked back to his trailer and called the Kaye ranch.

"Hey, Caleb. How's it going?" Joel asked.

They exchanged pleasantries for several minutes. Finally, Caleb said, "I called to talk to Kaye, not you."

"I'm a Kaye."

"And I'm done talking to you. I'd like to speak to your sister."

"I'm hurt." The feigned outrage turned to laughter. Joel shouted, "Sis, pick up."

"Can you take a message?" she called back.

"No, I can't take a message. I think Caleb wants to talk to you."

Immediately, the extension picked up. "Hello."

Caleb closed his eyes, enjoying the sound of her voice. "How are things going?"

"It's a true test of my army training. I can see why Joel decided to sucker me into doing this. How did things go there?"

"When I got in that ring with Razor, waiting for the first rider and horse out of the chute, I felt a peace, a healing peace. Things went smoothly and all the cowboys wel-comed me back. It was like old times."

"That's good."

Her lack of enthusiasm confused him. "I talked to Jack Murphy, the rodeo stockman. There's been a delay, but he said he'd arrive next Friday morning. He should have feed with him, but the feed store in Peaster has volun-teered feed, so just remind them to have it there on Fri-day morning."

"I'll do it."

"How are you, Kaye?" He worried about her reaction to his being gone.

"I haven't had time to think. You can't imagine how crazy things are. But I'll say, though we've had a couple hiccups, folks have been generous. When plans change, people have gone with it."

"Maybe I should've stayed."

"It was nothing I couldn't handle."

That was his strong Kaye. "There's something I want to talk to you about when I get back." He wanted to spill his guts, but doing it for the first time, he wanted to be face-to-face with her.

"What?"

"When I see you in a couple days, I'll tell you."

The next day, the Saturday before the rodeo, local par-ticipants came to set up their booths. Most of the ranch-ers worked from sunup to sundown and didn't come to town in the middle of the week to socialize, or in this case, work setting up displays. Kaye arrived at seven and had a full morning.

"Kaye, are you here?" Billye called out.

"I'm in the office," Kaye replied. The door to the office stood ajar. Kaye looked at the clock. It was noon. No wonder her stomach rumbled.

Billye pushed the door open farther and walked in. Amanda, Stewart and Branigan came in with her. The office was almost too small for two women, two kids and an Irish wolfhound.

Kaye stood. "Hey, friends, are you here to decorate?"

"We're here to help Mom," Amanda piped up. "She needs our opinions."

Kaye smiled at the little girl. "I see. Do I need to go and unlock the booth?"

Amanda nodded. "Yeah, it's closed."

Kaye went back to the desk, saved her work and exited the program. She grabbed the keys Ken gave her yesterday.

As they walked, Amanda wrapped her hand around the dog's collar and he guided her. Wooden stalls lined the edge of the fairgrounds north and south of the stadium, and half were filled with people working on their displays.

"I wanted to see how I could present the boots Jason is bringing," Billye explained. "He called me last night and said he was driving in for the rodeo. He's going to bring a few samples of other work he's done."

They stopped before the first stand inside the fairgrounds gate. Kaye unlocked the door and showed everyone how the awning opened.

"Are you and the ladies' auxiliary happy with this location at the fair entrance? You'll catch all the traffic. Have you talked to them since you saw it yesterday?"

"I have and they're okay with it, but a few mentioned they wanted to stop by today. They have a lot planned."

"Sounds good to me."

Several other people showed up and wanted to look at their spots. When Kaye walked back to the front, Billye waved her down.

"Okay, I've seen what I needed to see." She turned to Kaye. "I can't get my brain around the fact that the famous Jason Kelly wants to come and give away a pair of his boots. He wants to personally draw the winning slip, and that way he can measure our winner."

"Perfect."

"Jason told me something interesting yesterday." Billye smiled, much like a cat who'd eaten the canary. "He told me you ordered Caleb a new pair of boots. He's bringing them with him when he comes to the rodeo. So what gives?"

Kaye wanted to shush her friend. "I ordered Caleb a pair of boots as a surprise," Kaye said casually, trying to throw her friend off the scent.

The kids were playing with the dog. "And why would you do that?" Billye's eyes twinkled with mischief.

"I wanted to do something nice for him after all the work he's done."

"Are you ordering Joel a pair of boots, too?"

"No."

"C'mon, friend. Spill the beans."

Kaye didn't want to talk to her brother or grandfather about what was going on in her heart, but it might be nice to talk to her friend about it. "I think— No, I know—I'm in love."

Billye squealed and threw her arms around Kaye. Her kids stopped and looked at their mother.

"It's okay, kids. Ms. Kaye told me something neat."

The kids went back to playing. Billye crushed Kaye in a bear hug. "I'm so glad." When she pulled back, she started to smile at her friend but straightened when she noticed Kaye's expression.

"Being in love should make you over the moon. Why aren't you dancing and smiling?"

"You're right. I should be giddy."

Billye waited. "But you're not. Why?"

"Caleb took the job in Oklahoma City."

"Did he just up and leave without talking to you?"

"No. The rodeo booker called Caleb two different times. He turned him down, but I encouraged him to go."

"And he did. What am I missing?" Billye gave her a look that said "c'mon."

"I guess I'm letting my experience with my ex color things. I'm scared."

"You think?"

Kaye felt stupid and insecure.

"Oh, sweetie, you need to stop worrying. I've met Caleb numerous times and I haven't ever heard anyone say anything bad about him."

"But what if he decides to continue on the rodeo circuit, gone thirty weeks out of the year?"

"Kaye, if I thought every man in this world was like my ex…" She shivered. "Thankfully, not all men are like him. Caleb, well, the man seems like the salt of the earth. He's the guy you'd want in your corner."

"Kaye, there you are." The ladies from the auxiliary society walked into the fairgrounds. "We want to see where we'll be and make plans. Hey, Billye."

Kaye pointed to the booth. "Right here, ladies. I'll leave you all to discuss how you want to decorate."

Those were the quietest moments of Kaye's day.

A continuous stream of people came by the fairgrounds the rest of the day, checking out eleventh-hour details. Laurie, Mike and Nan also stopped by and updated her on what their final numbers were. Kaye felt at home, dealing with all the different details. After fielding the twentieth call over the past couple hours, she hung up and looked out the office window and froze. The sky had darkened in a way that sent chills down her spine. Spring in Texas brought tornadoes, hail and rain. They could use the rain, but—

She raced out of the office and glanced at the rolling sky. In the distance, she thought she saw a funnel cloud dip out of the massive thunderheads. There were several people on the fairgrounds getting things ready.

Suddenly, the emergency-warning horns went off. Kaye heard Billye calling her kids. Billye ran toward the office.

"Have you seen Amanda and Stewart?" she asked.

"No."

"I told them they could play fetch with the dog, but I can't find them now." Billye shook with fear.

Kaye grabbed her friend by the shoulders. "You check out the area by your booth. I'll check the other end of the field where the stock pens are."

People scrambled to take cover. The wind kicked up and the sky turned a greenish black. Kaye raced to the other end of the fairgrounds, yelling for Amanda and Stewart.

"Here," a voice sounded on the wind.

Kaye looked around and saw the two kids coming up from the creek bed at the end of the parking lot. Amanda had her hand around Branigan's collar. Stewart held the other side of the dog's collar.

The wind nearly knocked the kids over. Kaye heard the telltale roar of the tornado. She raced to the kids and pulled them farther into the gully. "Lie down."

The kids stretched out and Kaye lay beside them, her arm across their backs. Branigan lay on the other side of Stewart.

Between the sirens and the roar of the tornado, Kaye couldn't hear the children's cries, but she could feel them shaking with fear. "Lord, let me keep these kids safe as I couldn't keep those women in Baghdad," she breathed.

Chapter Thirteen

Finally, after several minutes of sheer terror, the sirens quit and the air calmed. An eerie quiet settled around them, except for Amanda's sobs.

Kaye raised her head and looked over the edge of the incline. The tornado had only destroyed a couple booths. A door from someone's car rested in the middle of the parking lot.

"Is everyone okay?"

The kids looked up at her and nodded. "I want my momma." Amanda's bottom lip quivered.

Stewart hadn't cried, but his eyes were huge with fear. Kaye hugged him and kissed the top of his head. "You're okay."

Kaye stood up and lifted the little girl into her arms. "I know your momma wants to see you." She looked at Stewart. "You hurt anywhere?"

"No."

"You should be proud of yourself for holding your sister's hand. I'll have to let your mom know about how brave you were."

He gave her a tentative smile and they went to find their mother.

* * *

Caleb dialed the ranch number, praying that someone would answer. A large storm system had moved across Oklahoma about one o'clock in the afternoon, generating a couple tornados. The same system moved southeast into Texas, hitting the Dallas-Fort Worth area. The local TV station in Oklahoma City said the tornado had touched down in Peaster. The instant that story aired, he called.

"Hello."

Caleb hung his head in relief. She was safe. "You're okay."

"Yes."

"I saw the news report and freaked."

"Well, it did surprise us. It touched down at the fairgrounds but only damaged a couple stalls, then moved on. It's going to take a day or so to clean up. Billye and her children were there on the fairgrounds and were a little shaken up. How are you? The news said Oklahoma City had experienced some damage."

"It struck the parking lot of the coliseum. Several trailers were damaged, mine included." He didn't want to worry her, but she needed to know it was going to take a few days for him to get his trailer repaired.

"Are you okay?"

"I am. Thankfully, Razor and I were inside working. The repair shop up here doesn't think they can get to my trailer for a couple days, but I'll be back in time for the rodeo on Friday no matter what. If I have to, I'll rent a trailer."

"I'll count on that."

He'd be there no matter what. Working this rodeo had freed him and made him realize he had no regrets giving up rodeoing. The drive up I-35 had convinced him his traveling days were over. He wanted to stay in one place and wanted Kaye by his side. "How are you, really? Did you have any more flashbacks?"

"I'm fine. The sound of the tornado didn't trigger anything except getting Billye's kids to safety. I didn't freeze."

He knew the train sound of a tornado, had gone through a couple of them himself, and remembered the wind and pressure changes those monsters brought. If she'd made it through without a problem, it could only be a good sign. He heard what sounded like her choking back tears. "I was able to keep Billye's kids safe."

"I don't doubt that."

"We're going to work tomorrow to repair those damaged booths and do some cleanup. I think we should be ready in time for the rodeo."

"I'll be there. It's a promise. I won't let you down."

"I'll count on you."

He hated the delay, but he'd prove to her that she could count on him.

Kaye disconnected the phone but held the receiver to her chest. In the chaos of the afternoon and her concern for Billye's children, she'd gone through that storm—a tornado at that—without having a flashback. She hadn't even thought of the flashback until Caleb had mentioned it.

Thank You, Lord.

"You going to hang the phone up?" Joel asked from the doorway to her bedroom.

She put the receiver in the cradle.

"I take it that was Caleb. Anything wrong?" The tenderness in her brother's voice made her smile.

"The storm system that hit us struck Oklahoma City first and damaged Caleb's horse trailer. He needs to have it fixed before he can drive back. He promised he'd be here before the rodeo."

Joel's gaze met hers. "You can believe him, Sis. Caleb has a reputation of meaning what he says. Anyone on the circuit will tell you, Caleb's a man of his word. You believe me, don't you?"

"Yes." She believed Joel, but as much as she didn't want it, visions of her ex-husband filled her head.

He nodded, wrapped his arm around her shoulders and squeezed.

But as much as she wanted these doubts to go away, they still lingered.

Early Friday morning, Kaye stumbled out of her room to grab a cup of coffee and a piece of the coffee cake Nan had delivered yesterday. The woman wasn't giving up her quest to win Joel.

"Hey, Sis. This is the big day. Rodeo starts tonight." Joel grabbed his travel mug.

"It's D-day." Her stomach danced with excitement and anticipation, but mostly because she'd see Caleb.

He'd called every night that week, and last night he'd promised no matter what, he would be there either with or without his trailer. He'd also told her that he'd taken care of his part of rodeo business while away. He'd warned the stockman that if he wasn't there in Peaster to contact either Joel or Kaye.

Joel caught her arm, put his mug on the counter and folded her into a hug. She hugged him back, resting her forehead on his chest.

"Don't worry. Everything is going to be fine."

She pulled back. "I know the rodeo will be fine."

"That's not what I'm talking about. Have faith. Caleb will be here. He had a good reason why he was held up in Oklahoma."

"He had to have the trailer repaired."

"True."

Warning bells went off in her head. Joel knew something. "Want to share?"

"No." Joel grabbed his cup and filled it with coffee. He also cut a big piece of coffee cake.

"I could tell Nan you adore her cooking," she threatened.

Joel stopped in the doorway. "Nope, you won't do that." He took a big bite of the coffee cake.

"Don't count on that."

He shook his head and swallowed. "Sis, your heart hasn't changed. You don't do dirty." He went outside, whistling.

Kaye didn't know whether to feel outraged that Joel wouldn't talk or pleased at his backhanded compliment. Her cell phone rang, giving her no time to ponder. Someone needed something for the rodeo.

Caleb arrived in Peaster a little after nine-thirty Friday morning. He'd been on the road since five-thirty and had only stopped once for coffee and an egg-and-potato burrito. As he made his way south, he knew his final ride as a pick-up rider would be in this charity rodeo. He'd surprise Kaye, then tell her it was his swan song. He drove straight to the fairgrounds and spotted the rodeo rigs carrying all the stock animals driving into the fairgrounds. He waved at Jack, pointing to where he needed to park the vehicles. Caleb quickly parked his trailer and after unloading Razor and taking care of him, he helped Jack with the stock.

"I appreciate you stepping up to the plate, Jack," Caleb said as he led one of the horses into the corral.

"Not a problem, friend." He looked around at all the help that showed up. "I wish all my stops were this easy.

And I'll be able to stock up on feed with the help I'm getting here."

The generosity of the local merchants and their suppliers blew them all away. Caleb knew all the different congregations in the city had joined together for this single goal. Seeing the Christian walk in action buoyed his spirit. "They're good."

Once the animals were unloaded, Caleb wanted to find Kaye, but he turned around and was caught by George "Shortie" Landers, the pick-up guy who was to work.

"This is quite a shindig."

Caleb pulled Shortie aside. "I have a favor I want to ask of you."

"Sure, what is that?"

"I'm going to change up a few things." Caleb told him what he had in mind. Shortie agreed.

Kaye walked up and down the booths to make sure everything was in order. "Are your electrical connections working?"

"Ours seems to be messed up," Viola, the head of the PTA, answered.

Kaye hurried around the booth, knelt and worked on the tape holding down the extension. When she stood up, Billye was there with a rugged-looking cowboy. He wasn't hard on the eyes, and Billye looked like she'd run the forty-yard dash. Branigan stood between Billye and the stranger.

"I was just looking for you," Billye said. She peeked over the counter. "What were you doing down there?"

"Securing the PTA's electricity." Kaye nodded to the man with Billye. "Who do you have with you?"

"This is Jason Kelly, our boot maker."

Kaye offered her hand. "I am glad to meet you, Jason, face-to-face."

"Ma'am."

The ladies from the PTA oohed and aahed, with a couple giggles thrown in. Kaye thought they sounded more like teenage girls instead of mature women.

Billye nodded to the booth beside the PTA. "We're going to set up your display in the next booth, Jason."

Jason grinned. "I'll be the first booth folks see. That's good."

"We did that on purpose, but while you're setting up, let me borrow Jason and show him the schedule for when he is due to draw for the boots."

Billye's brows knitted into a frown.

"It's easier to do this now because it's only going to get more hectic as the day wears on." Kaye didn't wait for Billye to reply but pulled Jason toward her small fairgrounds office. "Did you bring the boots?" Kaye nodded to several people as they walked.

"Yes, ma'am, I did." This man was a true cowboy, polite in his manner.

"I feel like I'm still in the army with all the ma'ams."

He smiled, and if another cowboy didn't have her heart, she could see possibilities here. Except Jason had eyes only for Billye. "I have the finished boots in my truck. Would you like me to get them for you after we go to the office?"

"No, let's walk out to your truck and I'll put them in my jeep so I can surprise Caleb without my brother or Gramps spilling the beans. I'll have your money for you tomorrow."

"I trust you. I don't think Joel Kaye's sister would short me. Besides, if you bought those for Caleb, I know I will be paid."

Reputation, Kaye thought. Your name and your honor still went a long way out here. "We'll do the drawing for the custom boots between the bareback riding and the calf-roping on Saturday night. I'll have the office open so you can take measurements of the winner."

At Jason's truck, he pulled a box off the floor behind the driver's seat and opened the lid. The two-tone boots were exquisite, and the leather felt smooth and soft. Jason was a master.

"You are a genius. They're beautiful."

"Thanks. I'm blessed to have my passion pay."

"I'm glad you contacted Billye and she brought the idea to me, but you could've called any one of the board members."

A lopsided smile appeared on his face. "It gave me an excuse to call her. I've been looking for one for a while."

Immediately, Kaye understood what Jason was implying. "Does she know?"

"No, but I'm going to make it clear this weekend."

"I hope you like kids. And dogs." If this man objected to either, their romance wouldn't last long.

"I love kids, and Branigan and I get along just fine. He knows I bring him treats."

"Ah, a smart man."

They parted ways and Kaye rushed to her jeep and stashed the boots.

Hurrying back inside, she saw Joel and Caleb over by the cattle pens. They laughed and joked. Both men seemed to come to life in this atmosphere, which only reaffirmed what she'd observed earlier.

Kaye stilled.

Was that it? Did both of the men have the rodeo so far in their blood that anything else paled in comparison? Did Caleb and Joel feel alive only in this atmosphere?

A chill swept over her soul.

* * *

"So how was Oklahoma City? You miss the excitement?" Joel asked Caleb. He'd seen Caleb talking to the other pick-up man and pulled Caleb aside when the other man left.

"Boring. Lonely. My last paid rodeo."

Joel's jaw dropped. "You sure?"

"I am. I have my eyes on something else and someone else."

Caleb looked up and saw Kaye coming down the aisle. He was zapped again. The woman had that effect on him. He still couldn't believe his feelings for her and that she returned them. He'd wrestled this past week with loving her, but then he read what Paul said in *1 Corinthians 13* on how unselfish true love was. What his mother practiced was not love, and the results her children lived with were disastrous. True love never brought the fruits his mother reaped.

Kaye was waylaid by someone, who waved wildly. They exchanged several words, then she turned and shrugged at them. "Wait," Caleb protested, but before he could run after her he heard, "Hey, Caleb."

He turned toward the voice. Caleb scanned the workers. When several people moved, Caleb saw the familiar face.

"Sawyer." Caleb met his brother halfway and enveloped him in a big hug. "You're here." Seeing his brother only added to Caleb's joy.

Caleb pulled his brother along with him. He looked around for Joel, but in the press of people he'd disappeared. "Did you register for any events?"

"No, not yet."

"Good, because since this is my final rodeo, I'd like you to ride pick-up with me. If you feel uncomfortable doing it, though, I can have Shortie work with me."

"Sure, I'll help." Sawyer studied his brother. "You look different. Do I see stars in your eyes? And was the woman I saw you eyeballing a minute ago Joel's sister?"

"It shows?"

"Yeah. Looks like you've been smacked between the eyes."

Caleb thought about it. "Good description."

Sawyer grinned. "Where's that ornery horse of yours?"

Caleb laughed. "You want to hear something amazing? Razor adores the woman."

Sawyer stopped and stared at his brother. "You're pulling my leg."

"I hope you'll see for yourself. You got a place to stay tonight?" Caleb scanned the crowd, seeing if Kaye had had a chance to come back.

"I planned on the moon."

Caleb's head jerked around. "What?"

"No need for me to say more. You've been bit."

Local volunteers, contestants and vendors poured into the fairgrounds, readying the facility for the start of the rodeo at five o'clock on Friday night. Finals would be held the following night. The kids' events would be on Saturday afternoon.

Kaye didn't have a moment to think, and last-minute details kept her from finding Caleb. The instant she solved one problem, another person needed something else or had a question. She didn't lack for help, but they all wanted direction or to check with her. Two radio stations had reporters on site and two broadcast stations were also there doing background pieces. She occasionally saw glimpses of Caleb and they waved.

The mayor pulled her aside. "It looks like we're going to be a success."

She surveyed the grounds teeming with people. "I think you're right."

"I'll admit, I was annoyed with your brother for drafting you. I thought he was ducking his responsibility. But I think I owe him an apology. He knew what he was doing."

The mayor's words encouraged her. The day rushed by, giving her no time to sit down. By three-thirty, her stomach rumbled. Kaye walked by the booth Billye had fixed up. It looked amazing. Also, the ladies' auxiliary had brought a small bookcase and displayed handmade quilts on it.

Kaye's stomach complained again, and the ladies heard it.

"I'm going to run over to the restaurant and grab a bite to eat."

Billye rushed out of the booth and linked arms with Kaye. "I'll come with you." Branigan whined.

Billye hurried back, picked up the dog's leash and locked arms with Kaye and dragged her off the fairgrounds down to the Sweet Shop. "They have great lunches here, and she was going to stay open late today."

Kaye got the three-salad lunch and Billye had a cookie and latte.

"Oh, this is so good." She forked another bite of chicken salad. "Where are your kiddos?"

"With my neighbors. They'll be coming tonight."

Billye's eyes twinkled.

"What's up?" Kaye asked, knowing her friend had news. Kaye waved her fork. "And don't try to say nothing. Remember, I can read you as well as you read me."

"Jason Kelly. He held my hand and asked if I'd like to go out after the rodeo was over." Billye sat back, shaking her head. "He wants to go out with me."

"I believe he likes you."

"That can't be it." Billye shook her head. "That can't be. My ex—"

"Forget about that man. He'd want you to be miserable. Trust your heart. Maybe God is bringing a blessing into your life." The words intended for Billye rang loud and clear with Kaye. She'd been talking herself out of happiness, worrying and doubting Caleb. Maybe she should allow her heart free rein. Maybe God was restoring her wounded soul. And maybe she ought to find Caleb and give him a kiss.

Chapter Fourteen

Kaye sat by Gramps and Joel in the stands. The bareback riding was the next event up. Looking around at the overflowing stands and listening to the laughter and roar of approval, Kaye felt humbled. This rodeo exceeded her expectations.

"Sis, you pulled it off." Joel wrapped his arm around her and squeezed. "I knew you'd do a better job at this than me." He wagged his eyebrows at her.

"Right. And do you have a bridge you want to sell me, too?"

Gramps elbowed Joel. "She's got you there."

"Could be." Joel stood.

Kaye looked up at her brother. "Where are you going?"

"I need to get ready. I'm going to be in the tie-down event."

She looked up at Joel. "When did you sign up for that? And why didn't you tell me?"

"I talked to Mike this afternoon and he said I could enter. I paid the entrance fee just like everyone else." He looked away, but there was a smile on his lips. Before she could respond, he walked down the steps whistling and disappeared from view.

The announcer came on the PA. "Ladies and gentlemen, we're going to start the bareback riding. Welcome our pick-up rider, Caleb Jensen, and his brother, Sawyer."

Kaye nearly fell off the aluminum bench in the stands. "Did you know Caleb and his brother were going to ride pick-up, Gramps?"

"No. I'm as surprised as you."

Caleb rode into the arena. He nodded in acknowledgement of the applause.

Kaye's stomach tightened. Caleb had said he wanted to talk to her about something. Looking at Caleb's face, there was a smile there. He was enjoying being back in the ring. Her hope splintered.

As they watched the bareback riding, Caleb's skills amazed her, always ready and always there for the cowboy. When the third rider made his time, Caleb positioned himself by the rider and the man grabbed on to Caleb and slid off the bucking horse, landing on his feet.

Kaye's fingers gripped the bench. By the fifth rider, Kaye felt like she'd been run over. She slipped out and walked down the steps.

"Kaye."

Kaye looked for who called her name and saw Sophie McClure. Sophie had run the equine therapy ranch in Albuquerque where she'd spent the past few months strengthening her legs. A little boy sat by her and Sophie held a baby in her arms. Kaye moved to sit by Sophie. The women hugged.

"What are you doing here?"

"Zach's competing in team roping with his brother, Ethan. No one would know he lost his leg while in Iraq. Nothing stops him now. How are your legs?"

"Good, but I'll say that after today, they're tired." Kaye

smiled down at the bundle in Sophie's arms. "This is your new one?"

"This is Kitty. She's two months old."

The buzzer went off, and Kaye looked at the floor of the stadium, eager to see where Caleb was.

"Which pick-up guy has your attention?"

Kaye's gaze snapped back to Sophie's. "So it shows?"

"I recognize the look. Saw it on the faces of both sisters-in-law. I probably wore that look, too. So which one is it?"

"Caleb is on the bay horse."

"You'll have to introduce us later."

The last rider in the event was announced. Kaye's cell phone vibrated. It was Ken, the fairgrounds manager. "I need to see you now," he said. "Let's meet in the office." With that she left the stands.

When Kaye found Ken, he'd taken care of the problem, but he wanted to talk to her about the calf scramble. After that, other vendors caught her and she didn't come up for air for the next hour and a half. She'd just stamped out the last problem and was walking to the office when she saw Sawyer.

"You and your brother are good," Kaye told him.

"Thank you. And you're Kaye. Caleb pointed you out as we passed earlier today. I'm Sawyer, the younger, better-looking brother."

She laughed. "It's nice to meet you. Do you ride pick-up, too?"

"Not usually. Me, I'm an events guy. I like shaking it up with the riding and roping, but Caleb's the best at what he does. That skill fed us, kept a roof over our heads and helped put me through college."

"I know."

Sawyer stared at her, eyes wide. "Really?"

"Was that a secret?"

"No. It's just that you're the only person he's told that."

"You mean the only girl."

"No, the only person."

Sawyer's words rattled her, but they gave her hope.

"I rodeoed summers, trying to get as much money as I could for school, and had a part-time job during the school year to help with expenses. But it was Caleb's earnings that put me through."

Seeing Caleb from his brother's eyes only added to the man's appeal. He'd put others before himself, unlike the man she'd married who only knew his own needs.

"He's good." Pride rang in Sawyer's voice. "And he never complained about me getting the chance for a college degree. He wanted it for me." He fell silent. "He's always been the one who rescued me when—"

"He hasn't changed." Her flashback came to mind.

"What?"

"I've been on the rescuing end of your brother's attention a couple times."

Sawyer studied her, then nodded. "That I don't doubt. Now that he doesn't need to help me anymore, I know he has a dream to buy a ranch and settle down."

"You think he will?" If anyone knew Caleb, it would be this man.

"If he had a good reason—" his gaze focused on her "—I think he will."

She hoped that was true. "Good to know, but with all this craziness, I haven't even gotten to say hi to him."

"I think I know just where to find him."

Caleb walked Razor to his temporary stall. As he started rubbing Razor down, a woman appeared.

"You were good out there, Caleb."

His head jerked up and stared at June Walker, the wife

of the man his mistake put in the hospital. "June. How is Tag?"

She stepped to the metal railing that made up Razor's stall. "He's healing quickly. He wants to start riding again and wants to compete in the September rodeo in Billings."

Walking around Razor, Caleb felt his mouth go dry. "So he's doing okay?"

She nodded. "I want you to know that the doctors said that you saved him from being paralyzed."

"But he had broken legs and a ruptured spleen."

"True." Her lips quivered. "But he didn't have a broken back or some of the other injuries the doctor talked about. I just wanted to thank you for saving him. You see, if you hadn't saved my husband, he never would've seen the birth of his little girl." Her eyes filled with tears.

Caleb opened the gate and walked to June's side. She threw her arms around him. Her action took him by surprise, but she seemed so vulnerable. He gingerly patted her back, feeling like a duck in the middle of a pack of wolves.

Pulling back, she wiped her eyes. "I didn't mean to get sloppy on you." She chuckled. "Tag complains that I've become a real waterworks."

"That's okay, June. Sometimes guys are stupid."

She snorted a laugh. "Any woman could've told you that."

She wiped her eyes and gave him a kiss on the cheek.

"You'll always be my hero." With those parting words, she started off into the crowd. As she walked away, Caleb knew he needed to help Tag and June. "Wait, June."

She paused, turning toward him.

He came to her side and pulled out his wallet. He had the cash that he was paid in Oklahoma City. "Here. I want you to have this."

She looked down at the four thousand dollars. When

her eyes met his, they reflected her bewilderment. "I don't understand."

"I know with Tag being laid up, you've had expenses, so this is for y'all."

June's mouth quivered. "I can't—"

He shook his head. "Please, let me help. I had a wonderful church meet my needs when I needed it. I know you and Tag could probably use some extra money now."

Her eyes filled with tears. "Thank you." She leaned up and kissed his cheek.

Caleb felt a peace settle over his soul as June slipped into the crowd. Tag would ride again. And his wife credited him with saving her husband. He shook his head, but it was as if God was saying it was time to forgive himself.

"Okay, Lord, I get the message." As he turned to go back and finish grooming Razor, Sawyer appeared with Kaye.

He didn't say a word but walked to her and gave her a hug. "It's about time I got to talk to you." He pulled back and stared into her eyes.

"I know. Each time I get near you, someone needs me for something."

"Me, too. I tried looking for you, but—"

"So you rode pick-up with your brother."

"I wanted to do that for the charity rodeo. Besides, it was nice to have Sawyer work with me." He smiled down at her, wishing he could take her someplace private and say a proper hello.

Sawyer stood to the side, grinning like he couldn't believe his eyes. Caleb threw his brother a meaningful look, but before Sawyer could move the mayor said, "There you are, Kaye. We need you."

She gave him an apologetic smile, turned and left.

The mayor's need was a quick interview on a local radio

station. Afterward, as Kaye walked to the next event, she overheard a couple cowboys. Their words stopped her.

"It was great to see Caleb riding again."

"I saw him last weekend in Oklahoma City. He's lost none of his skill. I don't know why he took off, but I think he's got it straightened out because he's in fine form."

"Ya think he's going on to the rodeos in Waco, then San Antonio?"

"Of course. He's got rodeo in his blood."

As if a giant fist hit her in the stomach, Kaye fought to catch her breath as she grappled with the words she'd just heard.

At nine-thirty that night, Kaye, Joel, Mike, Laurie, Nan and the mayor stood in his office and counted the money from the ticket sales thus far. They were eighty percent of the way to having the money it took for buying all the grain.

"If we've grossed that much, I bet we'll sell more single-day tickets tomorrow," Mike said.

"And we don't know what each of the booths made and will add to our total. Things look good," Nan commented.

"I think we'll make our goal," Asa said.

The people in the room began to clap.

"Let's wait and see what the final totals are tomorrow night." Kaye added the word of caution. So far, things were looking great, but who knew about tomorrow. The mayor locked the money in the safe in his office, then the group left the building.

"Are you driving Gramps home?" Kaye asked Joel.

"Yup. You coming home, too?"

"No, I planned on staying with Billye so I could get here early and if anything happened in the middle of the night, I'd be close."

"Okay, sounds like a plan." Joel stopped in front of her. "What's wrong, Sis?"

"What are you talking about? The rodeo looks to be a success beyond our wildest dreams." She couldn't look her brother in the eye.

He gently raised her chin with his finger. "I know you. Something's eating you."

She leaned up and kissed his cheek. "Thanks for thinking about me."

He hesitated, studying her. Joel was one of the few people she couldn't hide her feelings from. He read her like a book. He'd been a rock when she'd gone through her divorce, coming to Fort Drum and cheering her up. And he knew how she'd ached after their parents had been killed. But she wasn't willing to talk about her fears.

Thankfully, he didn't push, but kissed her cheek and walked off to find Gramps.

Caleb and Sawyer stood by Caleb's trailer, and Gramps sat on the foldout steps.

"There you are, Joel. You ready to leave?" Gramps stood. "Where's your sister?"

"She's staying in town with Billye. Good news. We've almost made enough to purchase all the seed."

"I'm not surprised," Caleb said. "The people in this area are generous."

Joel pulled out his keys. "We'll be here as soon as we care for the stock. The pancake breakfast the church is planning is here on the fairgrounds."

"See you then," Caleb called out.

Once they were alone, Sawyer slapped Caleb on the back. "I like Kaye. She's impressive. Tell me, what are your plans?"

Caleb stepped up into the trailer and pulled off his hat.

"You want to sleep on the floor in a sleeping bag or the bed?"

Sawyer's eyebrow arched. "You're not going to answer my question?"

Caleb sat on his bunk. He could ignore his brother's question, but oddly enough, he needed to talk, and Sawyer was the right man. "You remember when we were kids, before Dad died, what was your dream?"

Sawyer stepped back, as if surprised by the question. He leaned back against the trailer wall. He frowned. "Why?"

"Humor me."

Sawyer studied his brother. "I remember watching Dad work his heart out, but it was never for his own place, and I didn't want any part of that. I wanted to be a rich oil man who was the head of his company, running the operations and telling folks what to do."

"But what was your dream, Sawyer? What did you really want to do with your life?"

He tilted his head and considered the question. "I saw problems at the ranch and stockyards where they loaded the cattle onto the railcars. I could see ways to make the cowboys' work easier and wanted to tell the guys in the stockyard. I did one summer, and the man just shook his head and went back to loading the cattle. But the guy with him paid attention and the next week, he implemented my suggestion. I guess that's why I got my degree in business management, specializing in turning companies around."

"Did you ever see yourself with a family?"

Sawyer took the three steps across the trailer and sat next to Caleb on the bunk. "Maybe before Dad died. Afterward, no. I didn't want anything like what we grew up with."

Sawyer had received the most beatings because he

would never keep his mouth shut and go along with garbage their mom's boyfriends dished out.

Caleb knew that his brother would need heaven's intervention to heal. "I remembered more of what life was before Dad died. Mom was good then. I wanted a family, but after what we went through, I didn't want to gamble." He started to tell Sawyer about wanting to become an astronomer but knew he couldn't burden his brother with that spoiled dream. "Lately, I've found God's changed my attitude."

"You sure it wasn't an ex-army captain?"

"You're right, but God can use others. You remember the hours Pastor Garvey helped us, talked to us and took us fishing and camping, quietly showing us what a real family is like? Watching those families in the church that helped us, I saw the vision of family the way we used to be. I want to try that with Kaye but wanted to make sure it was okay with you."

Sawyer grinned. "Absolutely. I think you need someone to share your ranch who's not your kid brother."

"Yeah, you're not as attractive as Kaye." He elbowed Sawyer, drawing a laugh. "When I saw Kaye, something happened. The woman is a force unto herself." Except when he'd held her in his arms, walking with her through the terror. "You've watched her today. Was she indecisive or did she need anyone else to tell her what to do?"

"No, it appeared she told them."

"You've got it. That woman's been through a lot, but there's a quiet strength in her. I always wanted a woman who was strong, and Kaye's that woman. It kinda made me nervous, getting what I wanted and not knowing how to deal with it, but it's wonderful, having a woman with strength. She covers for me when I screw up.

"I used to think when you met *the woman* it would be

lightness and music. It was more like running into a brick wall, losing all my senses. I told her things about us growing up I've never told anyone else. She understood and didn't condemn. And she told me things, too, I'm sure she hasn't told anyone else.

"I wondered if I could settle down, but doing this last job in OKC, I knew I could give up the rodeo and vagabond life. I want to stay in one place. I want to marry Kaye."

Sawyer's eyes widened. "You're jumping into this with both feet—or boots." He smiled, amused at his clever pun.

"I am. I got the ring from a jeweler I know there in OKC. The lady and her husband raise horses. I found a little beauty I wanted to be my first horse for my ranch, besides Razor, and bought her. I thought I'd give that horse to Kaye as a wedding gift."

Sawyer's expression, eyes wide and mouth open, nearly made Caleb laugh.

"You're serious? Really?"

"I'm going to pop the question when this shindig is finished and she doesn't have a million things to think about."

Sitting forward, his elbows on his knees, Sawyer looked at his brother. "I'm glad for you, bro. You've given up so much for me, and I want you to enjoy your life." He stood and pulled Caleb into a bear hug, slapping him on his back. "I knew something was up when you looked at Kaye. I almost fell over when I saw the expression on your face. It nearly scrambled my brain."

Caleb couldn't help but grin. "I'd hoped for someone, but never expected."

"It's amazing what God can do."

Chapter Fifteen

Billye had reserved a room at the B and B in town, not wanting to drive the twelve miles outside of Peaster to where she lived. She'd offered to share her room with Kaye. Her children were camped at their best friends' houses for the night.

"Well, I knew you could pull it off." Billye walked out of the bathroom and climbed onto the twin bed.

Kaye nodded, feeling she'd lost.

"What's wrong?" Billye's eyes bore into Kaye. "You should be grinning ear to ear. We blew the socks off this place. Everyone is talking about how brilliant you are. And Caleb— Wow, watching him… That's it. What happened now?"

"What makes you think anything is wrong?"

Billye got out of bed and sat next to Kaye on hers. "Sweetie, what happened?"

The image of Caleb riding in the ring, laughing with Joel and the other cowboys, hearing those cowboys, she knew he belonged to this life. "What makes you—"

Billye held up her hand. "I can read you, even if you weren't a captain in the U.S. Army."

She wasn't in the army anymore and could show this

old friend her heart. "Did you see Caleb ride? Teaming with his brother? They belong out there and seemed to come to life, just like Joel. I know Joel's dream was to go on the circuit and rodeo, but circumstances stopped him. Joel still has that dream. Does Caleb?"

"Did you ask?"

"No, but I've been down this road before, seen the signs."

Billye's mouth pressed into a thin line and her eyes narrowed. "Didn't we talk about this before and settle it? Caleb is nothing like your ex. What happened to throw you off?"

Like a slap in the face, Kaye realized Billye was right. Caleb was nothing like her ex. She was running on old hurts, was looking at old fears. "You're right. He's nothing like my ex."

Billye slipped her arm around Kaye's shoulders. "I'd be the first to point out if the man, your man, struck me as all teeth, phony smiles and a black soul. I'd be with you. But I don't get that feeling from him. He's a man who will do you right." Billye squeezed Kaye. "And if Caleb's heart wasn't set on you, I'd be tempted to go for him."

"What, and let that hunk Jason Kelly pine away for you?" Kaye wanted to laugh at her friend's expression.

"Well, no, but you know what I mean." Billye pointed her finger at Kaye. "Stop borrowing trouble, girlfriend. Where's that spunky Brenda Kaye that let nothing get in her way? Trust the man."

Later, as Kaye lay in the bed, staring at the ceiling, she had to admit that Billye was right. She was putting her ex-husband's sins onto Caleb. Caleb deserved to be judged as himself.

Just as she was falling asleep, her phone rang. She grabbed it and answered.

"I wanted to say good night and sweet dreams." Caleb's rich baritone washed over her, settling her heart.

Kaye glanced at the other bed; Billye gave her a thumbs-up, turned over and went to sleep.

"Good night to you, too."

"And congratulations are in order. Joel told us about how much we made."

"It was amazing."

"No, you're amazing. I won't keep you. 'Night."

Her heart light, Kaye ended the call.

"See, I told ya so," came Billye's muffled voice.

"You're right." Kaye fell asleep with a smile on her face.

The next morning, the entire town showed up for the pancake breakfast. The mayor, Joel and Mike Johnson were the cooks. The five-dollar donation covered the food and also added to the total money they raised.

Kaye, Nan and Billy spent the morning making sure everyone had enough coffee and juice and that things ran smoothly. Finally, the workers sat down for breakfast. Caleb and Sawyer joined them for coffee.

"How did you sleep?" Joel asked Sawyer.

"The floor in that horse trailer isn't too comfortable, but I've slept in worse places." Sawyer glanced at his brother and they traded a look.

Kaye could imagine the bad experiences that the brothers had gone through.

"'Course, I would've slept better if Caleb didn't snore so loud."

They laughed. The group talked of the things that needed to be done for the afternoon events at the rodeo. The calf scrambles were this afternoon, one for the kids and the other with the police and firemen competing against each other.

As they finished, the people cleaned up the table. Kaye walked to the temporary office on the fairgrounds to get her paperwork for the day. After she grabbed her clipboard, she turned and found Caleb standing in the doorway. Her heart jerked.

"I wanted to have a moment with you before the day took off." Caleb stepped closer. "How are you?"

"Fine."

He nodded his head.

"Watching you yesterday was an eye-opening experience. You are good."

He stepped closer. "Thanks."

"And I like your brother." Her stomach jumped like a puppet on a string.

"I'm proud of him."

"And he's proud of you. When he talks about you, I can hear it in his voice and see it in his eyes. You hung the moon for him."

His eyes widened. "We were a team growing up." He pulled her into his arms. "I didn't come in here to talk about Sawyer." He settled his lips on hers. Hope fluttered to life in her chest, and all her doubts seemed silly.

"Kaye," a voice called out. The mayor barreled through the door. "I've got a— Oh, I'm sorry to interrupt."

"That's okay," Caleb said.

"I'll wait outside." The mayor grinned and stepped back out the door.

"I'll be there in a second," she called out. Her forehead rested on Caleb's. "I've gotta go."

"Okay, but I need to talk to you tonight after this is over."

Her heart thumped.

He gave her a final kiss before she rushed out the door. What did he want to talk to her about?

* * *

Saturday's attendance dwarfed Friday's, blowing away all the organizers. The crowd cheered the calf scramble with elementary school kids. The duel between the firemen and police in their calf scramble followed, with the firemen winning the event. The chief of police declared the firemen cheated to the roar of the crowd.

The barrel racing followed the calf scramble. Erin Mackay from Tucumcari won the event. As Erin walked out of the ring, she thanked Kaye.

"I'm glad that I was able to participate in this event. Since you've done so well, I might want to talk to you later about how you organized things."

"I didn't do anything special, but I'd be willing to talk."

"Thanks. Our local rodeo is facing some problems, so I thought I might pick your brain."

"Absolutely. The more heads, the better."

Erin nodded and walked her horse back to his corral.

Next up was tie-down roping, or calf roping as her dad had always called it. Kaye saw Joel bringing his horse to the stadium. Her brother was in the finals of calf roping.

"Are you enjoying yourself?" Kaye asked. Her brother exuded happiness. Much like Caleb.

"Does it show?" Joel grinned.

"Yes, it does."

"I'm having fun, and what is even better is we're going to make enough money to help all the ranchers." Joel brushed her cheek with a kiss, then mounted his horse and rode to the arena entrance.

Kaye found her grandfather and they watched Joel in the calf-roping competition.

"Maybe, now that I'm home, Joel should try his hand at rodeo again," Kaye said as they watched Joel bring his calf to the ground. He flew off his horse and had the calf trussed up in eighteen seconds.

The thought had been rolling around her brain, especially after hearing him whistling the other night. How could she keep her brother from his dream? Caleb had also seemed to have the same reaction as Joel. That thought felt like a jab in the gut.

Gramps drew back and looked at her. "I thought you were going to go to school."

"I am, but I can work in the mornings before school and when I get home. Or we could hire someone, but I think we need to suggest it to Joel."

Gramps looked back into the arena. The next event, bareback riding, was up. Caleb rode in. "Or maybe there's another solution." His eyes hadn't left Caleb's form.

"Like?"

Gramps nodded toward the arena. "I think God might provide it."

Kaye looked at Caleb in the arena. Hope warred with doubt. Was there a possibility?

Kaye got up and rushed out of the stands the instant bareback riding finished and Caleb and his brother rode out of the arena. She hoped to catch Caleb. The men dismounted and started walking their horses toward the temporary stalls that housed the stock. Mayor Asa Kitridge stepped in her path.

"Kaye, we need you. We're going to draw for the boots by Jason Kelly. Billye wants you there."

Kaye looked back over her shoulder and saw a man approach Caleb and his brother. The man shook their hands.

"I wonder what Steve Carter is doing here," Asa commented.

"That's Steve Carter?" The head of the rodeo association who'd called Caleb.

"That's him. If you want a job on the rodeo circuit, he's the man you need to talk to." They started toward the arena.

"How do you know that's him?" Kaye asked.

"My brother wanted a job with his company, and I went with him prior to the interview. I was a character witness."

As Kaye stepped into the arena, a cold finger of fear ran down her spine. What did Steve want with Caleb? Maybe he wanted to talk to Sawyer. And maybe the moon was made of green cheese.

"Are you sure I can't lure you back as a regular, working for us?" Steve asked Caleb. "You were great out there. It would be a shame to lose you."

"I'm sure. I want to spend the next year setting up my own ranch, supplying you with animals."

"Does this have anything to do with what happened in Albuquerque? Because if it does, that was an accident. No one blames you. Your skill is badly needed."

"I'll admit it started that way, but in my weeks away, that's changed. There's someone I don't think would like me traveling, and the idea of staying in one place and making a home… Well, I want to give it a chance."

Steve's jaw went slack, making Caleb laugh.

After a moment, Steve shook off his shock and held out his hand. "I can't compete with love. If you ever want to work again, you have my number." He turned to Sawyer. "You were good, too, Sawyer. You wouldn't like to replace your brother, would you?"

Shaking his head, Sawyer said, "Thanks, but I think Caleb would pin my hide to the wall since we both worked so hard for me to get my degree. If I didn't use it… I can't do it. But if you need a consultant to help solve any management problems, I'm your guy."

"Thanks for the help with the feed." Steve started to turn away, then paused. "Who is the special lady?"

"The lady who pulled off this event." A sense of pride swelled in his chest. Kaye had done it. "I'm going to pop the question to her tonight after the rodeo."

"Best wishes, friend. I understand. My wife recognizes my traveling is part of the job, but I miss her when I'm on the road." He walked away.

"You've crossed the Rubicon." Sawyer grinned.

"Quit showing off your education." Pride for his brother's accomplishments filled Caleb. "Yup, the die's been cast and I'm committed to asking Kaye to marry me." *And Lord, I need Your favor.*

His cell phone rang. When he looked down at the caller ID, he saw Shelly Jackson's name. While he was in Oklahoma City, he'd bought Kaye a horse for a wedding present. "Are you nearing the ranch?" Caleb asked.

"We are. After we dropped off the horse, we thought we'd come to the charity rodeo. I like the cause."

"I'm leaving now." He disconnected the call and looked at his brother. "I'm going to be gone maybe thirty minutes. Cover for me if anyone asks."

Caleb made the drive out to the Kaye ranch in record time and beat the Jacksons by only five minutes.

"So this is where you've been hiding," Shelly commented as she got out of the truck.

"More like working."

Ralph, Shelly's husband, moved around to the trailer. "Quit giving the man a hard time. He's taking the plunge. Poor guy."

Shelly shook her head. "You're the happiest you've been, Ralph. So quit complaining."

Caleb's eyes widened, then he looked at Ralph and saw his contented grin. Opening the trailer, he walked inside and untied the mare. He backed her out and Caleb fell in love all over again. She was a beaut.

"Razor's going to be jealous," Caleb commented, and showed Ralph the stall for the horse.

After they got her settled, Shelly pulled a jewelry box from her purse and handed it to him. "Here's the ring you bought, and I tailored it the way you wanted."

He opened the ring box and saw an oval sapphire flanked by two oval diamonds in a platinum setting.

"I know your lady's going to love it," Shelly said. "And I've got the new saddle in the trailer."

Caleb carried the saddle in from the trailer and set it on the saddle stand at the end of the row of stalls.

"I'm eager to meet this lady who captured your heart. Talk around the rodeo was that there was no woman who could crack that armor around your heart."

"What?" Caleb looked at Ralph.

He shrugged.

"I never heard anything like that," Caleb said, wanting to defend himself.

"That's because the ladies talked about it among themselves. You were the man who was willing to be friendly, joke and tease, but if you wanted a forever after, move on. Caleb Jensen wasn't your man."

Ralph leaned in. "And if you want to know the gossip, Shelly's your girl."

She playfully swatted his arm. "Stop." She turned to Caleb. "Let's go. I'm eager to meet this exceptional woman."

Caleb wasn't sure what to think. He was just thankful his engagement presents were there.

* * *

The rodeo's success stunned everyone. Once all the stock and cowboys had been settled down, Asa announced a big celebration party at the fellowship hall of First Community Church. As Kaye walked in, a round of thunderous applause broke out. Kaye felt uncomfortable with all the praise. The mayor settled the crowd down.

"Well, folks, we pulled it off. We netted nineteen thousand more than we needed. Let's thank our rodeo team. Come up here, Kaye, Mike, Nan, Laurie and Joel."

Kaye didn't want a round of praise, but the team hopped up onto the stage. Kaye reluctantly joined them.

"These folks worked their hearts out and they deserve our admiration. I think we should do this on a regular basis."

Cheers greeted the mayor's response.

Each member of the team thanked all the people who worked with them. Kaye was the last one up.

"Actually, you should thank my brother, for he's the one who drafted me to take his place." Laughter followed her speech. Several people around Joel patted him on the back.

"And I also want to thank Jack Murphy for supplying the stock. If his company hadn't been willing to help at no cost to us, we wouldn't have done as well. Please come up here and take a bow."

Jack walked to the stage in the fellowship hall. "Thanks for the applause, but my boss, Steve Carter, who's standing over there with Caleb, eagerly jumped on the bandwagon, and thanks belong to him, too."

Steve waved to the crowd. Jack left the stage and Asa stepped forward. "Let's enjoy the party."

Caleb stood with Joel and Steve. The men were earnestly talking. What was going on? It looked as if Steve was pitching something. As Kaye made her way to Caleb, she heard Steve say, "The next rodeo is scheduled for Waco, then we make our way down I-35 to San Antonio. It's a good deal. Some of our top guys earn in the millions."

Kaye's footsteps faltered. That much money was involved? How could Caleb turn down that offer? Suddenly, there wasn't enough air in the hall.

She turned to escape outside when Billye caught Kaye's arm and pulled her into a hug.

"He kissed me," Billye whispered. When she pulled back, Billye's face reflected her joy. "And he asked me if it was okay if he could court me. Court me. How romantic and old-fashioned." She vibrated with happiness.

Kaye couldn't put a damper on Billye's moment. "And what did you say?"

"Is there any doubt?" She looked around the crowd. "The kids are sitting with him now. Amanda wants cowboy boots and he said yes. My kids like him and he likes them. Isn't that great?" She spotted them. "I gotta go, but I wanted to tell you my good news." Billye rushed off.

Kaye was happy for her friend, really, but her heart was breaking. She needed air and slipped out of the fellowship hall. She stood in the dark, looking at the stars. She tried to keep her fears at bay, wrestling with doubts and the wounds. When she fought back one doubt, another took its place. What was wrong with her? *Why, God, am I having these doubts? I prayed and gave them to You, so why am I having them again?*

Give it to God. She felt the words in her soul.

She looked up into the sky. She couldn't go back inside and see dreams of her and Caleb melting away. It was the coward's way, the way she'd coped before, but she couldn't smile at folks when her heart was breaking.

Out of the corner of his eye, Caleb saw Billye hug Kaye, then tell her a secret. He saw the direction Billye pointed and her face broke into a smile. Good for Billye. She was a nice lady.

"You listening, Caleb?" Sawyer asked.

"What?" Caleb turned back to Joel, Sawyer and Steve.

Sawyer grinned. "What's your opinion on what Steve said?"

"What do you think, being the college expert?" Caleb answered. His gaze wandered to Kaye.

"What I think is you're in love and you're not paying attention to our conversation."

Sawyer's words jerked his attention back to the group. Caleb looked at the guys. "Okay, guilty."

"So get," Steve said. "I'm not going to change your mind, and I think you have a more important conversation you need to have with a certain lady."

"Thanks, Steve." Caleb turned, expecting to see Kaye, but couldn't find her. He walked around the room, searching for her. He caught up with Billye and asked if she knew where Kaye was.

"No, but she was acting weird when I talked to her a few minutes ago."

He raced outside and saw Kaye's jeep driving out of the parking lot. It would take too long to hook up the horse trailer and follow her. He raced back to the reception and found Sawyer. "I need to leave and I don't have time to hook up the horse trailer. Can I use your truck and have you bring Razor back to the ranch?"

"Your horse goin' to behave?"

Caleb didn't respond, but his brother took pity on him. He pulled out his truck keys and handed them to Caleb. He rushed off.

"Bro, I need your keys," Sawyer called out.

Caleb stopped, pulled the keys from his front jeans

pocket and tossed them to Sawyer. "Just tell Razor Kaye's waiting. He'll behave."

Sawyer's expression was priceless and he wanted to savor it, but he needed to get to the ranch.

On her drive back to the ranch, Kaye couldn't hold back the tears. Several times, she wiped them from her eyes so she could see the road. She'd dared to believe, and it looked like she'd lost again. The pain was too much.

Are you sure?

Kaye looked around, wondering if she'd heard right. Oh, she was losing it.

She parked in the driveway, pulled Caleb's boots from the backseat and walked into the house. Placing the box on the kitchen table, she found a piece of paper on the kitchen counter and wrote, "For Caleb." She propped the note against the boot box and walked out to the barn, hoping to take Midnight on a ride. The bright moonlight bathed the countryside with golden light. When Kaye opened the barn door, she started to Midnight's stall only to freeze several feet inside the barn. A beautiful bay horse stood in the next stall by Midnight.

The horse greeted Kaye with a soft whinny.

"Hello, gorgeous. What are you doing here?"

The bay stuck her head out. Kaye knew an invite when she saw one and rubbed her muzzle.

The bay had a black mane and tail, along with four black socks.

"She's a gift," Caleb said.

Kaye whirled and faced him.

"Why'd you leave the party?" He moved toward her and stretched out his hand toward the bay.

"I was tired."

His eyes narrowed. "That's not the real reason you left."

"No. I just couldn't watch you and that bigwig rodeo guy talk. You're going out on the circuit again, aren't you? Go. If you got the itch, don't let me stop you. Once a rodeo man always a rodeo man." She felt small and churlish, but she wouldn't go through waiting for a man to come home again.

"What? What makes you think I want to go on the road again?" He appeared genuinely perplexed.

"Someone ID'd the man who was hanging around you all afternoon and when Jack thanked us, he gave Steve credit, too." She tilted her chin up. "And I heard him make you an offer. He wants you to come back."

"I had already turned him down earlier, but he sweetened the offer. If you would've hung around a little longer, you would've heard me turn him down again."

"Why'd you do that?" A tiny ray of hope sprang to life in her heart.

"Because I don't want to travel that road anymore."

"But you're so good."

"Thank you, ma'am, but you see, rodeo was a means to an end for me. It kept Sawyer and me fed, a roof over our heads and money to put my brother through school. Ask me what my dream is." He stepped closer.

"What's your dream?"

"I want to own a ranch and share it with a beautiful girl, and I don't mean this beauty here." He rubbed the bay's neck. "This little lady is a gift to that special woman I want to share my dream with. Why don't you head over to that new saddle—" he pointed to the saddle on the stand next to the stall "—and look in the right saddle bag?"

Kaye had never seen the saddle before and did as Caleb suggested. Her fingers closed around a velvet jewelry case. She pulled it out and opened it. There, in a platinum setting, was an oval sapphire flanked by two oval diamonds.

Her eyes widened as she looked up at him for an explanation. "What's this?"

"For such a smart woman, you ask some dumb questions."

Kaye's eyes widened and she covered her mouth with her hand.

"I came to this ranch to think about my future. Tried to figure it out. My belief in myself was shaken and I didn't know what to do. Then you showed up, and my heart went crazy. I love you, lady, and I want to make a life with you. Will you marry me?"

Her dream stood before her. She looked at the ring, then back at Caleb. "Yes, I'll marry you."

He drew her into his arms and kissed her. "I'm going to prove myself to you, lady. All I ask is for a fair chance."

His request cut across her heart. She'd judged him wrongly but promised herself and God she wouldn't do it again. "I promise."

"Good. Why don't we go tell your family our good news?"

Joel and Gramps were pulling to a stop. Sawyer drove Caleb's trailer.

The men piled out of their truck.

"The lady said yes," Caleb announced to the group.

"I knew it. I knew it," Sawyer said. "When I saw that 'look' on his face, I knew he was a goner."

"What look?" Caleb asked.

"That dumb look like you just ran into a wall."

After the laughter had died down, Kaye pulled Caleb inside. "Look on the kitchen table."

Caleb saw his name on the box.

"Open it."

The men gathered around and watched as Caleb pulled

off the top of the large box. Inside were the new boots that Jason had made.

Caleb carefully lifted one boot out of the box.

"By Harry, that's one smart-looking boot," Gramps said. The men looked at her.

"I had Jason make them for Caleb since the last set of boots that he made were looking a little worn." Caleb placed the boot in the box and reached for Kaye.

"Aren't you going to try them on?" Gramps asked.

Caleb looked straight into Kaye's eyes. "Nope. It will be a perfect fit."

Epilogue

Three weeks later, there on the fairgrounds, Kaye and Caleb were married. The arena had been decked out in flowers and bunting. The entire town had decided that Kaye deserved an extraspecial wedding and had brought fresh-cut flowers from their gardens and new greenery from their yards.

The ladies' auxiliary group had white netting and bunting they'd strung between posts they'd brought from the church's drama department. The Sweet Shop donated the cake and another church provided the reception food.

Kaye had found her grandmother's wedding dress that had been carefully stored in a cedar chest. Since her grandmother had only been five feet, the dress looked cocktail length on Kaye, so they cut and hemmed it. Kaye had a wreath of flowers in her hair.

Charlie Newman, along with the pastor from Kaye's church, would officiate.

Sawyer and Razor were Caleb's best man and groomsman, while Billye and Midnight were maid of honor and attendant. Amanda and Branigan were flower attendants. Caleb looked fabulous in his Western suit and new boots.

As Kaye walked into the arena, escorted by Gramps

and Joel, she felt a sense of peace and coming home. She wasn't going to have to look for her future. It was here, in Peaster with Midnight, Razor, Gramps and Caleb Jenson— the husband of her heart.

As she walked in, she saw the stands were full of friends and neighbors. Caleb stood in the middle of the arena, next to Pastor Tom and Charlie Newman, waiting for her.

She remembered nothing of the ceremony but the joy in Caleb's eyes. When he kissed her, the stands erupted in cheers.

The reception was held on the fairgrounds. After an hour, Caleb pulled Kaye aside. He kissed her, then whispered, "I love you."

She would never tire of hearing that. "I love you, too."

The past two weeks, as her joy increased, she'd watched the life drain out of her brother. When she'd prayed about it, a plan formed in her brain. "I'd like to float an idea by you."

Caleb smiled. "Okay."

"What if we didn't try to find a ranch, but stayed at the Kaye ranch?"

"You might have too many men with opinions."

Anticipation raced through her. "Not if we encouraged Joel to try to fulfill his dream and go back on the rodeo circuit. We could help Gramps until Joel came back. I watched him, Caleb. His face lit with joy at the rodeo. He gave up so much for me. I want to give him back his dream now."

Caleb cupped her face with both hands. "You are an amazing woman, Kaye."

"Brenda."

His brow shot up.

"Brenda's finally come home and made peace."

"Good, because this cowboy has also found home." He kissed her again.

"C'mon. Let's go tell my brother he's free to pursue his dream, 'cause Brenda's found hers."

"Yes, Brenda."

That name sounded so good. *Thank You, Lord.*

* * * * *

Dear Reader,

Captain Brenda Kaye captured my imagination the minute she appeared in *Redemption Ranch*. She was taking equine therapy for the injuries she received in Iraq. Well, each time I went to write Tyler and Beth's story, Brenda popped into my head until I promised her a story of her own.

So who could take on this determined lady? One morning as I read our local paper, there was an article on a man who made his living by being the pick-up rider in the rodeo for saddle-bronc riding and bareback riding. The pick-up man gets paid for each rodeo he works. The cowboys pay a registration fee, but if you aren't in the top riders, you don't make money. The minute I read the article, I found my hero. Caleb is a man who's struggled with life and is at a crossroads in life, as is Brenda.

This story was an emotional one for me as well as my hero and heroine. I hope their stories will touch you as much as they touched me.

Leann Harris

Questions for Discussion

1. Kaye came home because she had the "gut feeling" she needed to. Has that happened to you?

2. Kaye ran away from hurts and memories she didn't want to deal with, yet she had to face those hurts once she was home. Has that happened to you or someone you know?

3. What did you think of Caleb? His background?

4. Have you ever heard of pick-up riding?

5. Joel dumped the charity rodeo in his sister's lap. What do you think of his actions? Has someone else managed to do that to you? How did you react?

6. Kaye decided to take her experience with PTSD and help others. Do you think this was a good decision?

7. Were you surprised when Caleb told Kaye that was his first official date?

8. What did you think of Caleb's desire to care for his brother?

9. Caleb blamed himself for the accident that injured the cowboy he pulled off the horse. Was it reasonable to blame himself for the accident? Have you tried to take responsibility for something beyond your control?

10. Guilt was a driving force for both Kaye and Caleb. Were they unrealistic in their thinking?

11. What did you think of Caleb's dream?

12. Kaye realized what her brother gave up because of the accident that killed their parents. What did you think of Kaye's actions of freeing her brother to pursue his dream?

13. Have you ever been involved in a charity event? How did it make you feel? What did you learn from it?

COMING NEXT MONTH FROM
Love Inspired®

Available March 18, 2014

THE SHEPHERD'S BRIDE
Brides of Amish Country
by Patricia Davids
Desperate to save her sister, Lizze Barkman turns to formerly Amish Carl King for help. Will she fall for the one person she's forbidden to trust?

A FATHER IN THE MAKING
Hearts of Hartley Creek
by Carolyne Aarsen
Nate Lyster thought he'd never have a family of his own. But beautiful widow Mia Verbeek and her children could change that—if she's willing to make room for the handsome cowboy.

RESCUED BY THE FIREFIGHTER
by Gail Gaymer Martin
Fireman Clint Donatelli had shut the door on relationships. But when he comes to the rescue of pretty Paula Reynolds, will he give love a second chance?

CLAIMING THE DOCTOR'S HEART
Charity House
by Renee Ryan
Olivia Scott is at a crossroads in her life. So when handsome doctor and single dad Connor Mitchel and his twin girls capture her heart, her new path might just be becoming a mother and wife.

PINE COUNTRY COWBOY
by Glynna Kaye
Abby Diaz has returned to Canyon Springs to mend her past. But when she meets charming cowboy Brett Marden, could he be the key to her future?

FINALLY A MOTHER
by Dana Corbit
State trooper Mark Shoffner is happy to reunite Shannon Lyndon with her long-lost son. Can he persuade her to let *him* in her heart?

REQUEST YOUR FREE BOOKS!

2 FREE INSPIRATIONAL NOVELS
PLUS 2
FREE
MYSTERY GIFTS

Love Inspired

A wave of terror washed over Morgan Smith when she heard the tapping at her window. Someone was outside the caretaker's cottage. Had the man who'd tried to kill her in Mexico found her in Iowa?

Though she'd been in witness protection for two months, her fear of being killed had never subsided. She'd left Des Moines for the countryside and a job at a stable because she had felt exposed in the city, vulnerable. She'd grown up on a ranch in Wyoming, and when she'd worked as an American missionary in Mexico, she'd always chosen to be in rural areas. Wide-open spaces seemed safer to her.

With her heart pounding, she rose to her feet and walked the short distance to the window, half expecting to see a face contorted with rage, or clawlike hands reaching for her neck. The memory of nearly being strangled made her shudder. She stepped closer to the window, seeing only blackness. Yet the sound of the tapping had been too distinct to dismiss as the wind rattling the glass.

A chill snaked down her spine.

Someone was outside.

If the man from Mexico had come to kill her, it seemed odd that he would give her a warning by tapping on the window.

She thought to call her new boss, who was in the guesthouse less than a hundred yards away. Alex Reardon seemed like a nice man. She'd hated being evasive when he'd asked her where she had gotten her knowledge of horses. She'd been blessed to get the job without references. Her references, everything and everyone she knew, all of that had been stripped from her, even her name. She was no longer Magdalena Chavez. Her new name was Morgan Smith.

The knob on the locked door turned and rattled.

She'd been a fool to think the U.S. Marshals could keep her safe.

Pick up TOP SECRET IDENTITY wherever Love Inspired® Suspense books and ebooks are sold.

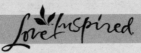
Carl King scraped most of the mud off his boots and walked up to the front door of his boss's home. Joe Shetler had gone to purchase straw from a neighbor, but he would be back soon. After an exhausting morning spent struggling to pen and doctor one ornery and stubborn ewe, Carl had rounded up half the remaining sheep and moved them closer to the barns with the help of his dog, Duncan.

He opened the front door and stopped dead in his tracks. An Amish woman stood at the kitchen sink. She had her back to him as she rummaged for something. She hadn't heard him come in.

He resisted the intense impulse to rush back outside. He didn't like being shut inside with anyone. He fought his growing discomfort. This was Joe's home. This woman didn't belong here.

"What are you doing?" he demanded.

She shrieked and whirled around to face him. "You scared the life out of me."

He clenched his fists and stared at his feet. "I didn't mean to frighten you. Who are you and what are you doing here?"

"Who are you? You're not Joseph Shetler. I was told this was Joseph's house."

She was a slender little thing. The top of her head wouldn't reach his chin unless she stood on tiptoe. She was dressed Plain in a drab faded green calf-length dress with a matching cape and apron. Her hair, on the other hand, was anything but drab. It was ginger-red, and wisps of it curled near her temples. The rest was hidden beneath the black *kapp* she wore.

He didn't recognize her, but she could be a local. He made a point of avoiding people, so it wasn't surprising that he didn't know her.

"I'm sorry. My name is Elizabeth Barkman. People call me Lizzie. I'm Joe's granddaughter from Indiana."

As far as Carl knew, Joe didn't have any family. "Joe doesn't have a granddaughter, and he doesn't like people in his house."

"Actually, he has four granddaughters. I can see why he doesn't like to have people in. This place is a mess. He certainly could use a housekeeper. I know an excellent one who is looking for a position."

Pick up THE SHEPHERD'S BRIDE
wherever Love Inspired® books and ebooks are sold.